desiring his dating coach

a sweet romantic comedy

kristin canary

one

. . .

IF ADULTS HAD STARING CONTESTS, I would be the queen.

But right now, inside the conference room at Jamison and Associates, I finally have a worthy opponent—although "worthy" is a term I use loosely.

Miranda Jamison (aka my boss, aka the Wicked Witch) stands at the front of the room, her lithe fifty-something-year-old body tucked and nipped to perfection, her narrowed violet eyes zeroed in on me. "You cannot be serious, Kayla."

The modern-chic space—with its plush carpet, large oak table, and floor-to-ceiling window that gives a gorgeous view of San Diego Bay—suddenly feels a lot warmer. A lot smaller.

But it doesn't matter that someone definitely turned up the thermostat in here or that the table is surrounded by twelve other attorneys (all men).

To break eye contact is to concede defeat.

So, rather than shrinking like some sort of wilted flower, I cross my arms over my green silk blouse and black blazer, doing my best to look intimidating despite my rather petite 5'5" frame. "I stand by what I said. If you don't settle that case ASAP, Mrs. Lincoln has no hope of getting custody of her children."

Miranda's not-a-gray-hair-in-sight brown bob shifts as she cocks her head and studies me like a spider must observe its next meal. But news flash, sister. I'm nobody's lunch. She may have pushed me around for the last seven years when I was desperate for a job so I could repay my massive law school student loans, but those puppies have been paid off for two months now. I am so done with holding back while Miranda berates me and gives all the promotions to my male colleagues —even when they don't deserve it.

Oh yeah, did you hear the part where Miranda and I are the only female attorneys at the upper-crust divorce and family law firm she owns? You'd think that would bond us together. Instead, it seems to have put me in her constant crosshairs. And lately, it's only gotten worse.

A smile curves across Miranda's unrealistically smooth face. At her age, there's no way she shouldn't have a few wrinkles. I wish she'd let them show instead of BOTOX-ing the crap out of her forehead, nose, mouth, and who knows where else. It would make her appear more human. (Although we all know that appearances can be deceiving ...)

"What does everyone else think? Do you agree with Ms. Clark? Should we just abandon our client in her time of need, when she's come to us for assistance?"

Daniel, another attorney who has been vying for an open junior partner position alongside *moi*, leans forward in the seat next to me. The air is thick with his expensive cologne, and I can't help but admire the cut of his Armani suit. Like all Jamison and Associates attorneys, he knows the importance of looking one's best at all times (even if there's an unfortunate and hefty price tag attached to the requirement). And with his rocking bod and styled blond hair, he does. Those muscles bulging beneath the suit coat aren't hurting anything either.

Then he opens his mouth and all the charm vanishes. "I think your plan to double down and push back is a brilliant one," Daniel says, grinning at Miranda like she invented Cross Fit, which he pretty much talks about nonstop because it's his "favorite hobby." (Sorry, but exercise is not a hobby—it's a necessity, and only a psycho would say otherwise.)

All around me, the men mumble their agreement. Looks like I'm standing alone. Again.

A snarky reply is on the tip of my tongue, but I bite it back. Yes, I may refer to Miranda as the Wicked Witch around my friends when I'm frustrated, but I also recognize that she *is* the boss. So even though she's done absolutely nothing to deserve it, by default I will do my utmost to show her respect.

Which means, for now, I drop eye contact and clench my teeth as Miranda covers a few other items from the agenda. My phone buzzes on the table and I peek down at a text from my mother.

Your father called. Again. He really wants me to give you

his number, so here it is. I'm only giving it to you so he will stop calling me, because apparently blocking his number does no good. Do with it what you will.

For the last three months, the dad who left when I was a kid has been trying to weasel his way back into my life via my mother. I swipe the notification away and focus on the meeting because I refuse to give the man another thought, another minute of my time. I've wasted too many years on him already.

Miranda finally dismisses the group to our afternoon midweek work. Thank goodness, because my standing coffee date at Java Awakening with my best friend and roomie Evie is calling my name. I snag my purse from my office then head toward the front lobby.

Jennifer, the receptionist who has been working here for a little over a month, waves hello from her desk. "How was the meeting today?"

I arch an eyebrow. "Swell."

Jennifer laughs. "That good, huh?" Taking a quick peek around the empty lobby, she leans closer. "How goes Project Get-Me-a-Date?"

"That name needs some serious work, you know." But I laugh in spite of myself, allowing the tension from the meeting to roll off of my shoulders and away. "I'm still looking for the perfect guy for you. Don't worry. I'm a pro."

My housemates tease me about my ability to know which celebrity couples (and real-life ones) will make it and which won't, and I've helped set more than one friend up on dates.

Jennifer nibbles her bottom lip. "Just remember, I don't look like you."

"So?" She's right—my shoulder-length highlighted brown locks are nothing like her bright red curls, and her tall frame has a lot more curves than mine—but she says it like it's a bad thing. I don't get it, though, because she's beautiful and sweet and any man would be lucky to have her. I just haven't found him yet.

But I will not give up, because that's not something I do.

Jennifer looks down at her desk. "*So* … the guys who would say yes to *you* wouldn't even glance at me twice."

"Believe me, you don't want the kind of guy who would say yes to me."

"You mean rich, sexy, and an amazing kisser?" She looks at me and sighs. "No, I don't want a man like *that* at all."

I laugh. "How about conceited and only interested in one thing? No, you deserve a guy who actually wants a relationship, who cares about you on a deeper level, who sees you as more than someone to have fun with." Although honestly, I like fun. Fun keeps things low pressure—and it keeps my heart safe. "And those guys can be sexy and good kissers too."

Not that I'd know from experience, which has shown that most guys who are actually worth having a rela-tionship with are intimidated by my strong personality. Even though they might say they want a woman who doesn't play games, apparently they don't like it when a woman is tooooo blunt or has no filter or calls them on their crap. (Go figure.)

"Well, I'm sure if anyone can find such a mythical unicorn for me in San Diego, you can." Jennifer grins as three of the male attorneys breeze past us, laughing and joking like good old boys. Daniel is one of them, and as he opens the glass front door, he turns and winks at me before leaving for what I assume is a late lunch.

"Looks like someone has a crush on our Kayla," Jennifer says as she fiddles with some pens in a container on her desk.

"Gag me."

"What? He's dreamy. With the way his eyes are always on you, I'm shocked he hasn't asked you out yet."

"Oh, he has. Three times." One of them just this morning, in fact.

"And you said no? Why? Not your type?"

"He's handsome, sure, but I can't stomach his arrogance." And there's an even bigger reason I won't go out with him. "I also don't date co-workers."

Unlike Evie, who recently fell in love with a guy she worked with for ten years, I find the whole idea much too messy. There are too many potential variables to take into consideration, too many things that could go wrong.

Too many things outside of my control.

"Hmm. Okay." Jennifer considers me. "By the way, in addition to finding me a date, do you think maybe you could give me a makeover and help me like you helped your other friend?"

A few months ago, Evie became my special project. We worked on building her confidence in order to land a promotion—and in the process, she also landed her boyfriend, Connor. "Of course I'll help you. Let's figure out a time to get together soon."

"Thanks, Kayla. You're awesome." She points at the clock on her desk. "You'd better go if you want to make your coffee date. Say hello to that yummy barista for me while you're there."

I lift my eyebrows. "Who, Josh?"

"Mmm hmm."

Yummy, huh? Jennifer went with me last week to pick up drinks for a client meeting, but she never mentioned that she thought Josh was cute. Although with his boy-next-door good looks, I'm not surprised. "Maybe he would be a nice match for you."

"I don't know. It looked like he might be into you."

I wave the suggestion away. "That's just silly." The guy is quiet and sweet, and I'm kind of the opposite of that. I doubt he'd be attracted to my particular brand of crazy. "You two, though … I'll have to see if he's single."

"But—"

"See ya!" I turn on my heel to head out the door, but hear a hideous sound behind me—the clearing of a throat.

Her throat.

"Kayla."

In slow motion, I round to find Miranda standing in the lobby's opening. "Yes?" I say as sweetly as I possibly can. (I should be given some sort of acting award, people. My words are dripping with freaking molasses.)

"I need to speak with you." She crooks a finger at me

like I'm a naughty student being summoned to the principal's office. "Now."

"Can it wait? I'm supposed to meet ..." But my words die off at the pinched look on her face. I sigh and pull my phone from my purse, dashing out a text to Evie: *Wicked Witch wants to meet. Gonna be late. Will text when I'm on the way.*

Then I follow Miranda, my four-inch Jimmy Choos sounding my doom down the wood-floored hallway.

When we get inside her office, she closes the door and indicates that I should take a seat. "I assume you know what this is about."

"No, actually I don't."

She sits across from me behind her desk and steeples her long thin fingers together under her chin. Her features could be beautiful if she used her powers for good and not evil. Instead, she resembles a hawk with eyes narrowed and plump lips pursed (like a beak curled and ready to peck me to death). "It's true. There are *so many* things we need to discuss. Your insolence during today's meeting, for example."

My cheeks are blazing as bees start buzzing in my ears. She has no idea how much I held back during that meeting. Or maybe she does, and she's just testing me now.

But I will not explode. She's pushed me further than this and hasn't broken me yet. "I'm sorry you felt I was being insolent. You asked for my opinion, and I gave it." I keep my voice nice and controlled. Steady.

Take that, Wicked Witch. (What? I never said I was mature in my own head.)

She sighs. "Then there's the matter of your clothing. I thought we'd discussed last week how you were going to wear outfits that were more … professional."

What happened to women uplifting one another? Yes, we had a "discussion" last Friday, when she berated my clothing choices in front of the entire staff. I glance down at my blouse and skirt. The shirt is not low-cut in the slightest and the pencil skirt, while hugging my curves, goes all the way to my knees when I'm standing up.

It's not as if her clothes are much different. I just don't understand the double standard. Perhaps she can enlighten me. "About that—"

"But what I actually called you in here to discuss today is this. I have it on good authority that you continue to ask Daniel out, almost to the point of harassment," Miranda says. "And we just can't abide that kind of behavior here, Kayla."

I'm sorry, what? I shoot out of my chair. "I haven't asked him out. *He's* asked *me* out multiple times, despite multiple no's on my part."

"Even if that was true, I'm sure you encouraged him in some way or he wouldn't keep asking."

The utter gall of this woman. "And just how do you suppose I did that?"

"I believe I mentioned your clothing choices."

Oh, we're going there, are we? My hands become fists at my side. "So you think that if a man can't help but harass me, it's my own fault because of what I'm wearing—which isn't even unprofessional, I might add? What is this, 1950?"

"Please don't shout, Kayla." She's trying to hold back a grin. I can tell by the brightness in her eyes, the same one she gets when she's closing in on an opponent in the courtroom—like a shark on the hunt for wounded prey. *Well, I'm not bleeding, lady, so back off.* "I still find it difficult to believe that Daniel would make all of this up."

"Of course he's making it up. He's trying to take the junior partnership away from me!"

She laughs, a trill that burns a fire in my belly. "For that to happen, it would have to be yours in the first place. And, I'm sorry to say it, but at this time you are not one of my top choices for the position."

I sink back into my chair. "What?" Seriously? After all the hours I've put in, all the ways I've dedicated myself to this job, all the ways I've gone above and beyond, she doesn't even see me as a contender? What about the time I was working mere hours after I got my appendix out—all while still in the hospital? Or the time I canceled my vacation at Christmas to cover a last-minute case that no one else wanted?

Or the many, many all-nighters I've pulled when the co-workers *she* promoted didn't do their jobs?

I guess I shouldn't be surprised, though. Miranda has never liked me. And yet … "Why?"

The back of my eyelids burn, but there's no way I'm giving her the satisfaction of crying over this. *"Never let them see you cry, Kayla. It's weakness, pure and simple."* My mom's words from childhood wend their way inside me, bolstering me, feeding my determination.

"Are the things I've just covered with you not

enough reason?" She sighs, shaking her head like she pities me. "You are a brilliant woman, Kayla. I only wish you'd spend a little less time looking down on everyone else and a little more time doing your job."

I sit there, feeling like a concrete roller has just flattened me. How could she say that? She *knows* what it's like to be a woman in today's workforce, especially in the world of law—how we're expected to not only have it all together but appear equal parts fierce enough to win for our clients and yet somehow soft enough to nurture and build relationships.

But it only takes a moment for the spark of her words to ignite into a raging fire that consumes all of me. And I realize in this moment that I'd rather be fed to a sarlacc by Jabba the Hut than keep working for Miranda. I don't need this job anymore—not like I used to.

And I don't need her.

"I quit."

Miranda rears back—but how can she really be surprised? "Excuse me?"

"You heard me." I stand without even a wobble. Because yes, this is right. And I should have done it a long time ago. "This is a toxic environment. You're a sexist. And I'm done here."

two

· · ·

THE SHAKES finally begin an hour later, when I'm being escorted by security from the building, a box in my hands.

I huff. Security is just Miranda's way of trying to embarrass me one final time.

But my leaving? That's her loss, not mine.

I look up at the skyscraper behind me, its windows glistening in the late-afternoon July sun. The only thing I'll miss about this place is Jennifer and a few of my clients who I bonded with after winning their divorce cases. I'm done allowing others (aka Miranda) to dictate my happiness. Done with a job I didn't even really like. It's time to make my own happy.

If only I knew what that looked like.

I trudge to the parking garage a few blocks away. Thankfully, San Diego remains temperate year round and it's only seventy-something degrees today. If I was back in Phoenix where I grew up, I'd be a melted puddle of Kayla Juice on the sidewalk right now.

When I reach my red Prius, I pop the trunk and settle the box inside. There wasn't much to round up—a few photos of me and my four housemates, some motivational prints with quotes by Eleanor Roosevelt and Ruth Bader Ginsburg, some pens, and my favorite teal coffee mug.

Not much to recommend the place I've spent countless hours of my life since graduating from law school.

Sighing, I climb inside my car and the buzzing in my ears finally quiets. I am alone with my thoughts for the first time in a while—and I don't like it. So I blast my Katy Perry soundtrack and drive off singing "Firework" at the top of my lungs.

And I don't even have to think about where to drive, because I can't go home right now. I need to be out in the world, not sitting around with nothing to do but think.

In ten minutes, I pull up in front of Java Awakening, the coffee-shop-slash-bakery that Evie and I discovered a few years ago. This has become our spot—our home away from home. When I postponed with Evie earlier thanks to the impromptu meeting with Miranda and then told her I was ready to meet, she promised to join me as soon as she could rearrange a few things in her schedule. But her new associate publisher position at Evermore, a boutique publishing house that specializes in historical romance novels, has been keeping her super busy the last few months, so I'm not holding my breath that she'll be here anytime soon.

Well, it's not like I have anywhere else to be anymore.

What have I done?

No, no, no. Do not think about the fact you just quit your job. Do not feel anything except the anger over Miranda's mistreatment of you. That, you can dwell on. That will get you through today.

I climb from the car and walk inside the coffee shop, where I'm assaulted by the familiar sound of vibrating coffee grinders and the smell of delicious baked goods. As usual, the place is busy, with students and employees from surrounding workplaces taking up the black iron tables that sit against brick walls. Industrial-looking lights hang from the ceiling, and Sam Smith's *Stay With Me* plays on low over the speakers.

I approach the bar, where there's a massive pastry case and a new sign next to the register that says *Help Wanted*. The two baristas, who are a constant whenever I visit during the workday, glance up. Hannah is a cute Southern blonde with doe eyes, a large chest, and a tiny waist. She's stinking adorable and always friendly. Today, she tosses out a hello before heading through the swinging door behind the bar that leads into the kitchen.

And then there's Josh, who waves as I step up to order. "Hey, Kayla." He adjusts his thick black hipster glasses. "When you didn't make it in earlier this afternoon, I wondered if you were sick."

"Not sick. Just … delayed."

"I hope everything's okay." His brown hair is slightly mussed, almost like he just rolled out of bed or took off a beanie, and I can't help but smile at the T-shirt he's wearing underneath a long-sleeved flannel. It's a picture of the Death Star II and says *I knew it was a trap before it was cool.*

"I like your shirt."

He glances down, then quirks an eyebrow at me. "You know *Star Wars*?"

I run my tongue over my teeth, shrug. "A little." (Ha! I'm not sure I've ever told a bigger lie, considering I'm quite well versed in *Star Wars* lore and watch the entire series—yes, even the terrible "newer" movies with Natalie Portman—multiple times a year. But only Evie knows this about me. It's a secret I will take to the grave, because, hi, it's not exactly sexy and I have a reputation to uphold.)

"Hmmm." Josh has on his signature quiet smile, which always makes me wonder what he's thinking. "What can I get you today? The usual?"

A mocha? No. I don't want the usual. Today is not a *usual* kind of day. "Make it a caramel macchiato." I need an extra infusion of sugar and sweetness, stat.

"Bad day?" He rings up my order and takes my credit card.

"What makes you say that?"

After running my card, he hands it back to me. "You only veer from the usual on days you've had a particularly terrible run-in with your boss."

"Oh." Interesting that he has realized this about me, but he probably knows things about all of his customers. He just seems like that kind of guy. "Yeah, it hasn't been great." I attempt to stuff my card into my wallet, but it won't go in. Grunting, I shove until the lip of the card finally slides into the slot, but then it's stuck and won't go farther.

"Here." Without warning, Josh takes my wallet, removes the card, and places it in another slot—one not stuffed to the brim with other cards.

"Thanks." I take the wallet back and toss it into my purse.

Josh considers me for a minute. "I'll have that macchiato right up."

With a nod, I slide over to an empty high-top seat attached to one side of the bar. As Josh starts on my drink, I check my phone. Evie hasn't texted yet, which means I might be here a while. But I can't really be mad at her. She doesn't know that I just quit my job. That I have no means of income.

That I may have just blown my life into a million pieces.

I place my head in my hands and inhale deeply. Panic threatens to edge its way in, but I refuse to let it. *You are Kayla Clark, and you can handle whatever life throws at you.* Another gem of sage wisdom from my mother, told to me upon my seventh birthday when I was sad that my hamster died.

Genevieve Clark may be many things, including a kick-butt CEO of a marketing firm in Phoenix who is neither soft nor tactful, but a true maternal figure isn't one of them. Still, she helped prepare me for life in a harsh world, reminding me with her words and her example that maintaining control is the key to true happiness.

Right.

It's not like I was fired from my job. I quit. I finally wrested control of my life back from Miranda.

Rational Kayla: *Now what are you going to do about it?*

Emotional Kayla: *I don't know. I'm still thinking! Give me a minute.*

Rational Kayla: *Buck up, Princess. Time's a wastin'.*

Ugh, I hate Rational Kayla sometimes. She can be a real witch. But she's also right.

"Here you go."

I startle at Josh's words and his sudden presence right in front of me. He's holding my macchiato, the corners of his light blue eyes creased with obvious concern.

"Thanks." I take the drink from him and sip, closing my eyes for just a moment. "Mmm, that's perfect."

"Is everything all right?"

"I quit my job today." My voice holds a tiny tremble and I pray he doesn't notice.

"Wow. That's huge."

"It was time." My fingers trace trails in the cup's condensation. "My boss … she wasn't a nice person."

"Yeah. It didn't sound like she treated you right."

I assume he's overheard me complaining about Miranda to Evie more than once. And oh, yeah. Last week, I stormed in here ranting about the dress code "discussion" Miranda had with me. I think I embarrassed the poor guy when I asked him to confirm whether he thought my outfit was too sexy for work. Me and my big mouth. Sometimes I wish I'd been born with more of a filter. But then I guess I wouldn't be me.

"No, she didn't." Under-freaking-statement of the year.

He cocks his head. "What are you going to do next?"

"To be honest, I'm not sure." Pointing across the counter to the Help Wanted sign, I manage a smirk. "If I can't find any jobs, maybe I'll come work here with you."

Josh just stares at me until a funny look passes over his face. "I know you're not really serious, but if you …" Clearing his throat, he grabs a rag from the back pocket of his skinny jeans and starts wiping down the counter, which already seems spotless to me. "If you ever did need a job, I'd be happy to give you one. My uncle owns the place, but he's basically retired and I'm the manager."

"You are?"

He shrugs. "Yeah."

It's not a big deal, but how did I never know that he ran the store? Although I guess I don't know a lot about him, just that he's a good person. He's always giving smiles, making others feel good, asking them about their days instead of talking about his own life. It's what any good customer service employee should do—and yet, with Josh, it never seems like part of his job.

It just seems like … him.

I shake myself from the random thoughts, finding his gaze focused on me once again, probably to gauge my reaction at his sweet offer. After taking another sip from my straw, I flash my pearly whites. "Thanks, but I'll be okay. I took the job with Miranda when I was fresh out of law school and just happy to have a job in a rough economy. Now, I'll finally get the chance to figure out what I really want to do with my life. It'll be amazing."

He pauses for a moment until our eyes lock once more. "If you're involved, I have no doubt that's true."

"You're really too kind."

He shrugs. "Just being honest."

And there's something in his gaze that makes me shift in my seat—like there's more he wants to say but doesn't.

I hold up my drink, give it a gentle shake. "Well, thanks again for this. It's made my day better."

"I aim to serve." He dips his head in deference like I'm some sort of royalty, and it makes me laugh. He really is such a nice guy.

Which reminds me of my conversation with Jennifer. "Hey, Josh, are you seeing anyone?"

His jaw slackens. "Um, why?"

Oh gosh, he thinks I'm asking for myself, and apparently the thought is frightening. Poor man. "Sorry, it's just that I think you and a friend of mine would hit it off. If you're up for that sort of thing?"

I'm usually pretty good at reading people, but Josh's eyes shutter in that moment, deflecting the light and locking me out. "I ..." He coughs and turns to find a new customer waiting at the counter. Hannah is still in the back, probably taking a break. "Um. Sorry. I've got to go."

"Sure, no problem."

His brow furrows and he starts to step away, then stops. "I'm not seeing anyone, but there is someone I really like. So. Yeah. I don't think I'd be up for meeting anyone new right now." Then, before I can reply, he's turning to greet the new customer.

Huh. Okay.

I finish my drink and wait for Evie to show up, all the while watching Josh—not in a creepy way, but just like a scientist would watch an animal in the wild in order to make observations. Because Josh is an enigma, and it's not often that I can't suss out what another person is feeling or thinking.

There's just something about him that intrigues me.

And as I take the final sip, making sure I get every last drop, I realize something else—this time about myself.

I'm not angry anymore.

There's a peace that's somehow settled into the cracks that my earlier anger dug. And I don't know if it's this place or the freedom of being out from under Miranda's thumb at long last—or being around Josh.

Who cares why?

Rational Kayla is right—the why doesn't matter. I should just be grateful for the calm and focus on my next steps. On moving forward.

On finally becoming reliant on no one but myself for my happiness.

Easy peasy, right?

Yes, indeed-y, sweetie. (Ugh, I'm sorry … once the rhyming starts, I can't stop! It's a compulsion.)

All of that to say—I was born for this moment.

And I'm determined to crush it.

three

I AM *NOT* CRUSHING IT.

I'm doing the very opposite of crushing it.

Groaning, I bury myself even deeper in the blanket that's covering me as I lay on the bright blue couch in the living room. Most of my housemates are around somewhere, but they'll be in here for a Sunday evening girls' night soon.

I'm looking forward to the camaraderie. The last week and a half since quitting my job have been so strange. It's been a lot more sitting around and waiting and a lot less moving and shaking than I'd hoped. (And I've already watched *The Empire Strikes Back* on my laptop three times. Shhh.)

I hear Alexis, Lauren, and Shelby talking in the back bedrooms, but can't make out exactly what they're saying. Probably I should go join them, if only so I'm not sitting here like a pathetic mess in my strung-up bun, T-shirt, and sweatpants. But the couch is just so comfy. In fact, even though this room is an array of hues (Alexis is a graphic designer with a penchant for bright colors in all things, including her hair), I find it rather relaxing.

The air smells of popcorn. I'm just gearing myself up to grab the bag I just popped when the front door swings open and Evie steps inside wearing an old pink tank top and gray linen shorts—the same clothes as yesterday.

I arch an eyebrow. "Well, well, well."

Evie just bought an adorable bungalow a few streets away, but she's still living in the room we share here while she fixes up her place. Between that and her new job, I haven't seen much of her—especially since she left yesterday afternoon and hasn't been home for more than twenty-four hours.

"Well, well, what?" She places her purse on a hook behind the door, drops beside me on the couch, and steals half of my blanket.

"I thought you'd be home sooner."

"Connor and I spent all day painting the house."

I know she's telling the truth, because there are flecks of dried paint in her long brown hair and on her clothing. But I can't help teasing her. "And that required you to stay overnight?"

As I waggle my eyebrows, she swats at me. "I'm too exhausted to deal with your innuendo. We intended to paint last night, but watched the six-hour version of *Pride & Prejudice* instead."

"So *that's* what the cool kids are calling it these days."

"You're impossible." A smile curves her lips.

I laugh, and after the last week and a half of turmoil, it feels good. I've missed my bestie. Evie is the first real friend I've had in a long time. That sounds pathetic, I know, but after my dad left when I was nine, I hid myself away from most people. The only other person I opened up to was Brendan, the guy I dated my senior year of high school—and *he* broke my heart in a million pieces when he dumped me minutes after high school graduation.

So you can see why I spent the next several years focused on school and the things that I could control, like getting a good job that would provide a life of security. After doing my undergrad in Phoenix and moving to San Diego for law school, I graduated, started working at Jamison, and looked for a place to live that would allow me to save money and pay off my loans—all a part of my master plan for a happy, controlled life.

When I replied to Alexis's ad online looking for housemates, I scored much more than I bargained for. Instead of just a home, I got a best friend and a built-in family. Somehow, Evie drew me out of myself and got to know the real me.

But now, as soon as she finishes up her house renovation, she's moving out. And I know we'll still be friends, but it won't be the same when we're not sharing the same four walls. Then she's going to get married and have babies and forget about her best friend … aaaaaaand I'm getting needlessly ahead of myself now.

Pinching Evie's side, I refocus my energy on teasing

her. "Methinks the lady doth protest too much," I say in a singsong voice.

"Mmm hmm. So how goes the job hunt?"

"I see what you're doing, trying to shift the subject away from your late-night escapades with Connor. But sooner or later, you're giving me details, my friend." It's been a while since I've been on a delicious date myself, so I'm living vicariously through my friend at the moment.

"I'll offer this. He's a very good kisser." Evie giggles, and I know that's really all I'm getting out of her. Although knowing her the way I do, nothing more than some kissing and Mr.-Darcy-watching actually occurred. She's just fun to tease.

I stick my tongue out. "Fine, be that way."

She grins, then grows quiet as she studies me. "Seems I'm not the only one changing the subject. Surely you have some new leads on the job search? People would be crazy not to hire you."

I sigh and pick at some fuzz on the blanket. "No law firm in San Diego will touch me—not since Miranda blackballed my name."

Evie goes pale. "What? How do you know she did that?" She finds my hand, squeezes.

"It sort of became obvious when the tenth law firm I called for follow up gave me the same spiel about deciding to go in a different direction while they still had the job posting up on their site. But I finally cornered a friend of mine at another firm and he confirmed it. I'm not hirable in San Diego, at least as an attorney." I take a deep breath, hating my next words. "Which means I've started applying elsewhere."

"You can't move!"

"I don't want to, but I may not have a choice." The idea of leaving the first city where I've developed real community—a real home—twists my gut. But what other options do I have? Miranda has stolen even that from me.

Before Evie can respond, Lauren walks in dressed in yoga pants and a workout shirt, her brown hair down and shiny around her shoulders. "You ladies ready for a par-tay?" She shakes her tight booty and lifts her hand in the air. (The woman is a cycling instructor, and constantly full of playful energy.) "What are we watching tonight?"

"I hope something romantic," Evie says.

"Surprise, surprise." I roll my eyes, smiling, as my phone pings on the coffee table.

Shelby and Alexis filter in, both dressed in pajama pants and T-shirts. Alexis heads to her rack of DVDs underneath the TV mantel and squats. I'm distracted by her orange hair—when did she have time to change it from the green she was sporting just this morning?

"How about something action-packed. *Thor*?" she asks.

"While I'm all about Chris Hemsworth's abs, I'm with Evie. Something full-on romantic sounds good." Lauren heads toward the kitchen. "I'm going to grab snacks. Evie, wanna help?"

"Sure." My bestie pops up from the couch and follows Lauren.

Shelby takes a seat in the colorful patchwork chair next to the couch. "How's your day going, Kay?" She snags a piece of her short blonde hair as she looks at me and smiles. Even her candy-heart pajamas showcase the fact she's a sweet-as-they-come kindergarten teacher. At twenty-five, she's a bit younger than the rest of us, but there's an innocence to her that I feel a fierce need to protect.

"All right." My phone dings again and this time I lean forward to read the text. It's from Jennifer. She's checking in on me.

Jennifer: *The office just isn't the same without you. I wish you hadn't left. How is the job hunt going?*

Ugh, I don't want to think about that anymore. But Jennifer's texts remind me that I haven't made any progress on finding her a man since learning that Josh isn't open to meeting her. She didn't act all that disappointed when we met up on Wednesday for her first confidence lesson, but still. I promised her, and I'm failing in that promise.

I tap my phone, lips in a frown.

"Bad news?" Shelby squints at me.

At that moment, Lauren and Evie come back into the room, chattering and balancing bowls of popcorn, chips and salsa, and Reese's Pieces. They set the stuff down on the coffee table and then plop onto the couch next to me. Alexis is still busy examining the movies, mumbling to herself as she scans past those she doesn't want, pulling those that are possibilities.

Someday, when these women find their Prince Charmings like Evie did, all of this will be gone. I'll be sitting alone in a house or apartment of my own—hopefully in San Diego, but probably not. I rub away the ache in my chest at the thought.

Maybe I'll get a dog when the time comes. Dogs have a lot of things going for them. One, they're not cats (because cats are evil). And two, they're the most loyal creatures in the world. My dog would keep me warm at night and give me kisses—albeit slobbery ones—and I'd never have to worry about him leaving me if I "outshine" him or intimidate him or become too much for him to handle.

"Kay?" Shelby's face is definitely twisted in concern.

"Hmm?" Oh, right. The text. "No, it's not bad news. Just my friend Jennifer. I told her I'd introduce her to a good man since she's new to the area."

Evie hands me a bowl of popcorn.

I turn to her. "I even started with confidence lessons for her like I gave you."

"Well, they certainly worked in my favor." My friend pops a handful of Reese's Pieces in her mouth. "Just warn her about the power poses."

Rubbing my hands together, I cackle like an evil magician thinking about the confidence-boosting poses I forced Evie to practice day and night. "Those are fun." Then I tap my phone against my knee. "I've run through my list of guys over and over again, but I'm coming up empty."

"I know you'll figure it out." Shelby gives me an encouraging smile.

Oh, hey. "Eric is single, isn't he?" Shelby's best friend from childhood, Eric is going to start teaching at the K-8 school where she works this coming fall. He's been around our house quite a bit and is all the things Jennifer needs in a man. I can't believe I didn't think of him before now.

At my question, Shelby swallows hard. Interesting. We've all been saying that Eric likes her, but she insists it's not true. And she's never given any indication she likes him in return—not until that little gulp.

But then she manages a crooked smile and nods. "As far as I know."

"Never mind. He's too …" At her pinched brows, I wave my hand. "I'm not sure they'd work. I'll figure it out eventually." Moving on. "So, what are we watching?"

We all move our attention to Alexis, who is standing at the front of the room with a stack of DVDs in her hand. "All right, I've got several options. Thought we'd go old school tonight." She holds up *Napoleon Dynamite* and raises an orange eyebrow.

"You're the only one who likes that weird movie," Lauren teases.

"That's because I'm the only one with real taste around here. But fine." Alexis holds up *Die Hard.* "Option B."

"Boo." Gathering a bit of popcorn in my hand, I toss it at her. "Evie and Lauren said they want something romantic."

Alexis puts a hand on her hip. "A guy kills a bunch of baddies to rescue his wife. That's romantic."

Evie laughs. "We were thinking more along the lines of a romcom."

"Figures." Our fearless leader (or the one who owns our house, anyway) discards a few other action movies on the coffee table. There are two left in her hand. "I want to say for reputation's sake that these are Shelby's —not mine."

We all laugh as she flips the remaining movie cases toward us: *Never Been Kissed* and *Hitch*. "You've got your pick between watching a teacher who gets the hots for a woman he thinks is a student"—a scrunched nose tells us her opinion about *that*—"or a ridiculous dude who has to hire a dating coach just to get the girl."

"I'm up for whatever." Shelby settles back against the chair, a throw pillow hugged to her chest. "I love both of them."

"Really?" And there's Alexis's curled lip. She's a hoot and a half, I tell ya.

Lauren also finds Alexis's reaction hilarious. "Oh, Lexi Lou, someday a man is going to sweep you off your feet, and then you'll love romance as much as the rest of us."

Alexis grumbles under her breath and shakes both movies to get our attention. "So which one?"

"Let's do *Hitch*. Will Smith is so handsome and funny." Lauren's face is serene as she pulls a blanket from the back of the couch and settles it onto her lap.

Alexis queues up the movie and we all sit back to watch. It's comfy and cozy and we laugh and joke as we watch. These women are my family. I don't want to lose this, but I'm not sure I have a choice.

Halfway through the movie, Evie suddenly scrambles for the remote and pauses the film. We all turn to look at her, and she's got this wild look in her eye as she turns to me. "Kayla. That's you."

"Who is me?"

"Will Smith. Hitch. That's you. It's what you do. What you did for me. What you're doing for Jennifer."

What is the woman raving about? I place my hand on Evie's forehead. Nope, she's not feverish.

But then Lauren gasps. "It totally is."

I cross my arms over my chest. "Can someone please clue me in?"

"A dating coach." Then Evie is grabbing my upper arms and shaking me so violently I think she must have lost it. "You could be a dating coach. You could start your own business. Grow it as big as you want to. And …" Her grin widens. "You wouldn't have to move."

"That's crazy." Are dating coaches even a thing? "No one would actually pay money to be taught how to flirt and kiss and dance." Would they?

No.

"Just because *you* wouldn't doesn't mean there aren't others out there who have tried everything to get the attention of someone they love and can't." The glow from the television puts a strange shine in my best friend's eyes. "You could help them."

"That is such a great idea," Shelby pipes up from the chair. "Kayla, you would be great at that. I could totally see it."

"I … I don't even know where I'd start." I mean, thanks to my undergrad in business, I know what it takes to run a company. But this kind of business would have to grow based on word of mouth. I doubt people would trust a Facebook ad for something like this, although you never know. People do buy the most random crap on Facebook sometimes. "Where would I even find clients?"

"I'm sure I could send some gym members your way," Lauren says.

"And you know I work with enough nerdy guys who are in desperate need of a makeover." Alexis quirks a smile. "Although I'm not sure you'd be able to encourage them to move out of their mom's basements, and that is a dealbreaker for most women."

The rest of my friends laugh, while I bite my lip, considering. But no. I went to school to become a lawyer. I don't want to give up on that dream just yet. Sure, I didn't like my job at Jamison and Associates, but how much of that was Miranda and the type of law we practiced there? Maybe if I could find something corporate and end up with a boss I love, I'd enjoy it more.

I snag the remote from Evie and bump her shoulder with mine. "It's a nice thought, but I don't think so."

Then I restart the movie and everyone quiets again, getting lost in the story—everyone except me. Because for some reason, I can't get Evie's suggestion out of my mind.

It would be bold. It would be ridiculous. I mean, I like a challenge, but this?

No way.

Taking a bite of popcorn, I force my attention back to the movie and away from the appealing prospect of working for myself. Helping people in the process.

Staying in San Diego.

No. I'm sticking with the plan—the one that has me applying to law firms in Los Angeles, even Phoenix (not that I really want to live anywhere near my mother again).

Because getting a traditional job means security. Control. Happiness.

What about this right here, right now? Isn't this happiness?

True. But this won't last forever. And when it ends, I don't want to be left with only memories to hold onto.

four

. . .

MY LUCK HAS CHANGED.

The evidence? I'm sitting across from Barbara McDonald, a senior partner at McDonald, Billings, and Associates in downtown Los Angeles. She's an older woman, maybe in her sixties, and—get this—she's smiling at me.

The day after the girls' night with my housemates, I received a phone call from Barbara's assistant asking me to come in on Friday.

Today.

We've just been through what should have been a grueling interview, but Barbara is the exact opposite of Miranda. Warm, encouraging—she'd make the perfect mentor.

And best of all? Her firm focuses on intellectual property protection and entertainment law. There's not a divorce case in sight.

She glances around the boardroom table, where two

other partners—a respectable middle-aged gentleman and a forty-something woman—sit. They both nod, and she flicks her smile back at me. "Well, Kayla, I think that if your references check out, you should be expecting a call from us very soon."

A shot of pleasure has me soaring, but then her mention of references brings me back to solid ground. "Oh." How do I put this delicately?

Keeping my chin notched upward, I pray that this won't ruin my chances at getting this job. "Look, I'm going to be honest. My ex-boss and I didn't see eye to eye on a few things. While I attempted to respect her way of doing things, I found them to be … unscrupulous. Unfortunately, I don't think she will give me a good reference."

The tiny wrinkles around her lips become more pronounced as Barbara frowns down at my curriculum vitae lying on the gleaming wood surface of the conference room table. But after scanning it for a second or two, her face relaxes and her eyes find me again. "I happen to know Miranda Jamison, and I agree completely with your assessment."

What are the freaking odds? The universe has heard my plea for a second chance and is answering. I swallow past a dry lump in my throat. "That makes me extremely happy."

"Me too." Barbara holds out her hand. "You should be hearing from us sometime after the weekend."

I shake her hand, then those of the other two partners before Barbara walks me out to the lobby. "Are you staying in town this weekend or driving back to San Diego?"

Since it's only two in the afternoon, there's still plenty of light. "I'm going to head home. Thank you again for the interview. I look forward to hearing from you."

"Of course. Thank *you*, Kayla."

As I walk from the building and find my way to the parking garage next door, I watch the hustle and bustle of downtown L.A. Even though San Diego is one of the top ten largest cities in America, it doesn't feel that big to me. Los Angeles, on the other hand, is a massive beast, with so many freeways it's easy to get lost even with a trusty GPS. Crowds clog the sidewalks and people move along like ants. And it's at least ten degrees hotter, a fact I discover when my armpits start sweating through my blazer on my trek to locate my car.

I finally get inside and, after punching my address into my phone, take off at a snail's pace through the city streets. It takes forever to get out of the downtown area—must be some event or an accident, or maybe it's just normal—and finally I'm on I-5 headed home. Ariana Grande and Lady Gaga keep me company on the three-plus-hour drive back.

And I try very hard not to think about how I might be making the reverse trip very soon, my things piled in the back of a moving truck. With every mile, something tightens in my chest. By the time I see the familiar San Diego skyline, I'm a windup toy. I can hardly breathe.

What is wrong with me?

But I know. I just don't want to admit it.

It would be crazy to turn down a solid job in my field. But it would mean leaving San Diego, and I just … I hate to be weak, but I don't know if I can do it.

One glance at my clock tells me it's nearing dinnertime, but a mental scan of my housemates' schedules reminds me that no one will be home tonight. Evie is working on her house with Connor. I'm sure they would be okay if I showed up to help, but I don't feel like being a third wheel tonight. Alexis and Lauren are both working late, and Shelby has plans with Eric and her family.

Once again, I can't abide the thought of going home to an empty place.

If I move, that will be my fate soon enough. Every night.

So once again, I head to the only other spot that feels like home. How pathetic that I'm so desperate for companionship that I'll go to a coffee shop where the only people I know are the employees paid to be nice to me.

Stop it, Kayla. You're going for coffee. A pick-me-up. Then you will go home, take a relaxing bubble bath, and read a good book.

Yes. That is an excellent plan. *Thank you, Rational Kayla.* (I'm really not a psycho who talks to herself all the time, guys. I promise. But desperate times, right?)

I pull into the Java Awakening parking lot, which is strangely empty of all but an old beat-up truck. Huh. After parking, I get out, walk toward the front door in my heels, and try the door.

It doesn't open.

I squint and peek inside. It's dark except for a light coming through the kitchen door window. Stepping back, I search the door for the store hours.

Nooooo. They closed five minutes ago.

Sighing, I turn to head back to my car but twirl at a scuffing sound—the opening of the door.

"Kayla?" Josh is standing in the doorway, looking confused.

"Hey." I walk back toward him. "I guess I've never been here this late on a Friday. Didn't realize you closed at six."

"No problem. Come on in." He holds open the door for me, nodding his head toward the inside.

I chew my bottom lip. "I don't want to make you late to whatever big weekend plans you have."

Josh chuckles, low and throaty, and for some reason, a shiver runs through me at the sound. What in the world? Sheesh. My emotions really are all out of whack today. Because this is *Josh*, the guy who I've seen several times a week for the last three years and never once felt an inkling of attraction to. "My big plans consist of going home to my tiny apartment and cleaning up after my three messy roommates. So please. Come in. Save me from myself."

His quiet wit makes me grin. "I don't know. It sounds really important. I'm not sure I should keep you." I lift my eyebrows as I tease him.

In an instant, his cheeks turn red at my perusal. "Yeah, I mean, whatever you think." Then he ducks inside faster than the Millennium Falcon jumping to hyperspace.

There I go, embarrassing the poor guy again. Guess he doesn't like to be teased. Noted.

I should probably leave him alone tonight, but my craving for java (and yes, for some company too) is greater than my desire to not foist myself on poor unsuspecting males.

So I follow him inside. He re-locks the door behind me as I take in the coffee shop. It's so different when no one is here. Gentle light spills from the windows onto the floor and out through the kitchen, but the other-worldly dimness of the rest of the space creates a cozy kind of vibe. No music plays, no machines whirr, no people chatter.

It's just … quiet.

Still.

Kind of like the guy standing beside me. The warmth radiates off of Josh, and when I turn, he's close enough to touch.

I step back, unsure if I'm the one who stepped into his airspace or vice versa. "I can pay you double for your trouble." (There I go, rhyming again. Oy.)

"No worries. I've already closed out the register, so this one's on the house." He shoots off toward the counter and I'm trailing him again, a protest on my lips.

"But I'm the one crashing your Friday night party."

"I won't make you anything if you're going to be stubborn about it." That mysterious smile of his makes another appearance—and it's maybe the lighting or the fact that we're completely alone for the first time ever, but it almost feels … different. Intimate. Meant just for me.

Get that coffee and get outta here, Kayla.

Right. "Fine." I point toward the coffee machines. "What do you suggest for a celebratory drink?"

He rubs his chin, which has a bit of a five o'clock shadow that lends him more of a rugged appeal than usual. "How about an iced white chocolate mocha? Bit of a twist on your usual."

"That sounds amazing. Yes. Do that, please."

"Coming right up." He gets to work, and as he does, I dig in my purse and stuff a twenty in the tip jar since I know he won't accept payment.

My eyes catch on the Help Wanted sign again. "You haven't found anyone to fill the job yet?"

He glances up from his spot at the espresso machine. "Nope." His hands get busy and I find myself a bit mesmerized by the precision in his fingers. And yet, there's a relaxation there too, as if he's got all night, like I'm not bothering him or intruding.

He's content to just take the next step. No real hurry toward the destination. The journey is what matters.

And wow, I'm reading far too much into the way the man makes coffee.

It's just coffee, after all.

"So," he says as he pulls the shot. "What are you celebrating?"

"I think I found a job."

"That's great." He quirks an eyebrow while assembling my drink. "But for someone who's celebrating, you don't sound all that excited."

How can the guy read me so well? Maybe there was

more disappointment in my tone than I'd intended. "It's in Los Angeles."

His body stills for the briefest of seconds—so short that I must have imagined the stiffened shoulders and taut torso. Then he hands me my drink and starts making something else, for himself, I'm guessing.

Maybe he won't mind if I stay for a few extra minutes.

"Oh?" he finally says.

"Yeah." Leaning a hip against the counter, I sip my drink (this may just become my new fave, because wow!) and watch him make an americano. We stand there in relative silence until he's done.

Then he rounds the counter and nods to a half-lit table in the corner. "Want to sit?"

I breathe a sigh of relief because I don't have to go home just yet to face reality. "Sure."

We walk over and sit opposite each other. He takes a drink, studying me over his cup before setting it on the table and gripping it with both hands. "You're really going to move?"

I chew the inside of my cheek and swing my legs under the table. "I can't find a job here. Not as a lawyer anyway."

"And that's what you really love to do?"

"It's what I trained for three years to do. What I've done for the last seven."

"You didn't answer my question."

I didn't, did I? "You're supposed to sit there and be the adorable barista that makes me delicious coffee, not challenge my decisions and make me second guess myself."

His features darken.

Oops. What did I say to upset him? "What's wrong?"

"Kayla, unless he's two years old, no guy wants to be referred to as 'adorable.'"

I laugh at his reaction—but oh, wait. He's not joking. Waving my hand in the air between us, I try to smooth things over. "I meant cute. You're cute. Sweet. Like a …"

At his blank stare, I swallow hard. I've offended him. Again. I cover my face with my hand. "Josh, just ignore me, okay? I'm a mess and not thinking clearly."

"It's fine, Kayla." He waits for a beat, then pulls my hand down to the table, covering it with his warm palm.

For a moment, I wonder if he's going to keep it there. I actually wouldn't mind if he did, because there's something comforting about his touch.

Instead, he moves his hand back to his side of the table. "I'm sorry things are so hard right now. Wish I could help you feel better."

"You are. Just by being a friend."

"Right." Josh glances away, toward the window. Obviously, he wants to get back to his scheduled plans —even if it's just cleaning.

"Um, well, thanks for this. I'll let you go."

"You sure? I kind of like the company."

I look at him, surprised. "Oh. Well. Me too."

We stare at each other for a long few moments, and I'm not really sure what we're communicating. All I know is his gaze is warm and soothing, like melted chocolate after a diet of carrot sticks and dry salad.

"So there was this woman who came into the shop today. She ordered 'the usual.' But it was the first time I'd ever seen her in my life." Josh proceeds to tell me about his day and all the crazy customers he dealt with.

At first, I wonder why in the world he's telling me all of this, but then I realize that it's his way of distracting me—which somehow he knows is exactly what I need.

My shoulders relax against the back of the seat and I kick off my shoes under the table as we volley quips and questions back and forth. Then he asks if I have any war stories of my own, and I launch into a few of my favorite battles with Miranda (only the ones I won, of course).

Before I know it, the light outside has dwindled and my stomach growls. I shake the last few tiny ice cubes around inside my drink, the rest having melted a while ago. "Thanks for this, Josh. I needed it. And I'm not just talking about the drink."

"Anytime." His tone is suddenly serious. "Hey, Kayla?"

"Yeah?"

Massaging the back of his neck, Josh watches me from behind his glasses. "You're obviously a strong woman who can make her own decisions, and I'd never presume to tell you what to do." He pauses. "But it doesn't sound like you want to take that job in L.A. Seems like you'd miss your friends, and I know they'd miss you."

"Life is hard, Kayla. Sometimes we have to be even harder to maintain the status quo." More long-ago words from Mom's life lessons drift into my brain.

I rub the corner of my eye. "You're right. But I don't know that I have a choice."

"There's always a choice." Josh's lips quirk a bit as his gaze shifts to his now-empty cup. "I was serious the other day about you working here if you want to. I know it wouldn't pay much, but maybe it could tide you over until you find a job in San Diego."

"Oh, Josh. That's so sweet of you."

His gaze is suddenly back on me—and piercing. "It's really not."

The hair on my arms lift in reaction. There's something he's telling me in that look, something I'm not sure of. "What do you mean?"

"Just that I'm being selfish in offering you the job."

"How is it selfish?"

He stares at the table. "Like your friends, I'd be sad if my favorite customer moved."

Favorite customer. The words play on a loop in my brain, and the warmth they create in my chest grows by the second.

I really should go. This is … confusing. "I'll bet you say that to all the girls." There. Teasing. I can do teasing.

"No, Kayla. I'm not offering anyone else this job until you agree to at least think about taking it."

My mouth falls open. "Who are you and what have you done with the Josh Gregory I know?" That is, the super-laid-back-non-forceful one. The quiet one. The one who listens but doesn't speak his mind.

Chuckling, he gathers our empty cups and stands. "All I ask is that you think about it. It could be exactly the opportunity you need to figure out your next steps. And"—he leans forward—"I'd be a much nicer boss than the Wicked Witch."

Then he winks (what the what?) and heads to the trash can to toss our garbage.

I blink away the crazy feelings swirling in my stomach—all stemming from that darn wink and none too welcome—and think about what he actually *said*.

Opportunity.

What if …?

No way.

But … maybe?

"What are you thinking right now?" Josh is back and sliding into his seat once more.

"Huh?"

"Your face. It looks like you sucked a sour lemon. Is the idea really so disgusting to you?"

"What? No!" I shake my head. "I was just thinking about something my housemates said the other day. They suggested I start my own business … as a dating coach, of all things."

I expect him to laugh, to tell me how ridiculous that is (not that he'd use those words—he's too nice). But instead, his features grow thoughtful. "Didn't you do something like that for Evie?"

Okay, the man is way too observant for his own good, because I know I didn't actually tell him about that. Maybe Evie did, though. "Yeah. And I mean, there are parts of it that sound really intriguing, you know?

I'd get to be my own boss. I'd get to help people. I'd get to build a business from the ground up, which sounds kind of exciting. I like a challenge."

"So what's the problem?" He shrugs. "Work here part-time or full-time and start your business on the side. You can always take a job as a lawyer in L.A. later if your business doesn't work out."

He's right.

The only risk is my time and energy. And yeah, maybe I wouldn't be quite as hirable if there's a gap in my resume, but I can easily explain that away.

Hmmm.

I tap my chin. "I don't know anything about being a barista. I've only ever made coffee in a pot—and that's because it was finals week and I was desperate."

"I'll train you myself. I'm sure you'll be a quick study. It'll be simple enough."

Okay, then.

Whoa. Dang. Am I really doing this?

I know there are a lot of people who dither around with decisions. Not me. I've learned to trust my gut, and right now my gut is screaming at me to try this.

Because I might always regret it if I don't.

So I extend my hand. "You've got a deal."

"Really?" His eyes widen.

"You're not taking back your offer, are you?" I tease.

"No." His hand engulfs mine, and there's that warmth zinging through my fingers again at his touch. "You're hired."

"All right, Josh." I smile. "Or should I say Boss? You win."

A grin—yes, a full-on grin—breaks out on Josh's face. "I kind of think I do."

A tiny thrill runs through me, not just at his words (which I pretend mean nothing to my cold, dead heart), but because I'm doing it. Taking control of my life. Finding my happy, which starts with staying in San Diego.

And also, apparently, working with Josh Gregory.

five

. . .

JOSH GREGORY IS A LIAR.

LI. AR.

Because being a barista is NOT simple or as easy as he implied.

Or maybe it's just me. Because I've already made I-don't-even-know-how-many mistakes in the first few hours of my inaugural day as a Java Awakening employee.

Like … I don't know. WEARING HEELS.

When Hannah arched her eyebrow at my choice in footwear this morning, that should have been my first clue. But my mother taught me to always look your best, whether you're going to the grocery store or presenting to a board of directors.

Apparently, that advice should not extend to standing on your feet all morning making coffee. Because I can't really feel my toes anymore and my leg muscles ache like nobody's business. And it's only been four hours.

I can't decide if I'm the world's biggest wuss or the dumbest barista on the face of the planet.

Plus, I really wish I'd opted for jeans and a blouse instead of my favorite red wraparound dress. It's what I like to call my *go-get-em* dress, and I felt like I could use an extra boost of confidence this morning—wrong-o! I've never felt overdressed at Java Awakening before, but that was as a customer. Now, as an employee, I've got completely the wrong vibe, a fact I'm all too aware of as a college-aged woman stares me down and tosses an order at me in what might as well be gibberish.

"Sorry, can you say that again?" I'm not normally this obtuse, but I'm used to getting detailed input about uniform codes and disclosure agreements, not milk preference and sugar substitutes. (One is not more important than the other. They're just very different, and it's taking my brain a hot minute to adjust.)

The customer flips her dreadlocks over her shoulder and huffs, repeating her order. I close my eyes, visualizing the words.

"I've got it, sugar." Hannah steps into my space and saves me in all her sweet Southern-talking glory—not for the first time today. (And sadly, probably not the last either.)

So just where is Josh Gregory, you might be wondering? Brilliant question. Apparently he forgot about a long-standing appointment with his uncle via video chat this morning and abandoned me on my first day in (which is five days after offering me the job).

Hannah said he'd be in soon, but for now, it's up to her to train me. Poor thing. She's already had to remake an order when I forgot to add the espresso to a guy's latte and again when I didn't add enough grounds to the machine and watered down an older woman's coffee. It happened during the flurry of the seven and eight o'clock hours, when Hannah's "training" was akin to tossing a toddler into the ocean and telling him to swim for the shore.

The Wednesday morning rush has blessedly died down a bit and I limp to the counter to take the next customer while Hannah makes a *half-whole-milk-one-quarter-non-fat-one-quarter-one-percent-extra-hot-with-split-quad-shots-no-foam* latte. Oh! Hopefully she doesn't forget the touch of vanilla syrup, three packets of Splenda, and three—not four!—sprinkles of cinnamon.

Sheesh, people. Some coffee orders are taller than the ridiculous requests made by my divorce court clients— the ones who had cheated on their spouses and asked for their half of an estate that happened to be protected by a prenup. What did they think I was, some sort of lawyer genie who could grant them a thousand wishes?

Shaking my head, I smile through the toe pain and take a nice elderly gentleman's order—a plain ole americano. Now that, I can do. After ringing him up, I take my turn at the espresso machine, being sure to grind the beans extra fine and add plenty of them because I don't want a repeat of Watergate (which is what I am calling the incident with the watered-down coffee ... yes, I'm here all day, folks).

I make sure to tamp the coffee extra hard, insert the

portafilter into the group head, and hit the button to brew the espresso (look at me and all my impressive barista-y lingo!). While I wait, I sing along with Taylor Swift and wiggle my butt just a little because who can resist dancing when "Shake It Off" is playing?

The espresso trickles into the cup below—and dang it!

It doesn't look right. Doesn't smell right either. That's because it's burnt.

I lift the cup to examine it more closely, to figure out where I went wrong.

"Everything all right?"

At Josh's voice, I jump and slosh the coffee all over the floor—and thankfully not all over him, though it missed him by about an inch. Growling and narrowing my eyes, I raise the mostly empty cup in my hands before waltzing to the trash can and tossing it in. "I guess things are all right—*if* you call your machine's rebellion against me 'all right.'"

Flouncing to the sink, chin held high, I snag a wet rag and return to clean up my mess (and if you think this is the first time I've done this today, I'll just let you keep on thinking that). I lower myself into a squat as best I can without flashing the entire shop.

"I'll have a stern talk with it later so this doesn't happen again." His chuckle from above fills my ear.

"I'm serious." I flick his legs with the wet rag (and smile with satisfaction at his surprised yelp) before swiping at the puddle of coffee, then use the counter to hoist myself back up.

After depositing the rag back into the sink, I toss a hand on my hip. "I did everything Hannah told me to do. Dose, level, tamp, flush, attach, brew. But this is the result."

Josh snags a new cup. "That's all correct, but you have to make sure you don't grind the beans too fine or tamp them too hard. It's a delicate dance. Let me show you."

Something about the way he says that sends butterflies scattering in my stomach.

What is my deal? Ever since our time together on Friday, I find myself thinking about him at the most random of times. But butterflies? *Really, Kayla? How original.*

No. I'm just nervous, that's all. I hate being bad at stuff, feeling incompetent. That's all this is.

Stepping back a bit, I watch him work his magic on a cup of coffee, his movements steady and sure, just like him.

"Does all of that make sense?"

"I think so. Let me try again."

And I do, while he watches and gives encouragement with each step I complete. He only has to correct me once, stilling my hands when I'm tamping. "I know you're used to doing everything at a thousand percent, Leia, but you can't put too much Force into it. Hang back just a bit."

"Leia?" And did he just make a *Star Wars* pun with the force comment?

There's his itch of a smile again. He shrugs. "I think you're more of a *Star Wars* fan than you let on."

"You do, huh?" I hip bump him out of the way while I finish tamping. "Hmm."

"Am I wrong?" This he says in a lowered voice, close to my ear, and it's got my body overheating.

What is *with* me today?

Shaking myself, I hook up the portafilter, hit the button to brew, and allow myself a teasing grin in response to Josh's prodding. "Stay on target."

An eyebrow arches behind his glasses. "We're too close."

"Stay on target." I wink and he laughs, because I've just exposed myself as a true fan by parroting a few lines from *A New Hope*, the original *Star Wars* movie.

And even though it's not a part of myself I ever share with people, it feels kind of nice to do so with Josh.

"Well, well, Kayla Clark, you are full of surprises."

I take a bow and watch the beautiful ribbon of espresso tumble into the mug below. When it's finished, he takes it and downs it in one fell swoop—brave man.

I bounce on my tiptoes. "Well?"

"It was … perfect."

Squealing, I throw my arms around his neck. Yes, I'm probably being much too enthusiastic about this victory, but it *was* a pretty frustrating morning and this is the first sign that maybe my plans to stay in San Diego and start up a dating coach business have a chance in hades at succeeding. (And yeah, I realize the connection between succeeding at making coffee and succeeding at running a business is thin, but I'll take the victories where I can.)

But I'm not gonna lie. Being in Josh's arms is not the worst feeling either, especially when he wraps his hands around my waist and squeezes.

Pulling back a bit, we stand there grinning at each other like fools, and I can't help but linger, moving my hands down his shoulders to his biceps.

Wowza.

He's not the biggest guy in the world, but how have I never noticed how defined his arms are? How strong he is?

At a cleared throat, I yank back to find Hannah staring at us from the register, her pretty mouth pulled into a frown.

Right. Not very professional of me to hug my boss like this. Or, you know, fondle his muscles. "Sorry. I just got excited for getting a drink right." I flash her a thumbs up but she just looks at Josh and turns back to the register.

He rubs the back of his neck, which has turned crimson. Then he looks at me. "Hey, I think it's time for you to take a break. I've got some paperwork for you to sign if that's okay?"

"Sure. Lead the way."

And just like that, we're back to some semblance of normalcy as Josh asks Hannah to cover for me and swings open the door between the front of the shop and the kitchen. Back here, the smell of pastry dough and chocolate is even stronger. I'm told the pastry chef, a woman named Linda, comes in super early every morning to make our baked goods. Apparently she will sometimes help out up front too if more than one of us has to call off.

There's a little table with chairs in the corner that Josh points to. "If you want to sit, I'm just going to go grab the paper from the office."

Back here, the noise from the front of the shop is a distant echo. There's a hum from the refrigerator, and it's much cooler. Or maybe that's just because I've stopped moving at a frenetic pace.

"Sounds good." I do as he says, breathing a sigh of relief as the pressure comes off my feet. And just because I don't think he will care, I ease off my heels. Much as I love dressing up every day, this obviously isn't going to work. I think I've got a pair of flats hidden away in the depths of my closet.

Josh is back soon and slides the paperwork across the table. "I forgot to have you fill this out last week. It's just a basic form for direct deposit if you want to do that."

I plant one elbow on the table and frown. "You didn't need to pull me off duty to do this paperwork. I'll have to take it home to get my banking information anyway."

"It seemed like you could use a breather, and every employee is supposed to get a thirty-minute break after working five hours."

"I've only been at it for four. You don't have to take it easy on me, Gregory."

"Eh, it's your first day." His smile warms me through as he leans back in his chair, arms behind his head. "So have you made any progress on your business?"

"Yep. I've registered for an LLC, done all the banking and accounting setup, created a business plan, and claimed all of my social media accounts."

He whistles. "That's a lot of things to get done in, what—five days?"

"I didn't sleep very much. When I get a plan in my head, I kind of get keyed up and just want to accomplish it as quickly as I can."

"Makes sense." Running his finger along a smudge on the tabletop, he fidgets in his seat a bit. "So what exactly does a dating coach do?"

"Confidence exercises, flirting practice, kissing tips, wardrobe makeovers, interpersonal skills, role-playing, behavior modeling. It just depends on what the client is trying to achieve."

He coughs. "Did you say role-playing?"

"Yes." I can't help but laugh at the way his voice catches. "For example, my client and I will go on a pretend date and I'll critique it. That kind of thing."

"Ah."

"What did you think I meant?" I lean forward and shoot him a teasing glare.

He squints and takes off his glasses, using the bottom of his flannel sleeve to clean them. "Do you have any clients yet?"

I'll allow him to get away with the change in subject, mostly because I'm not sure I want to hear his answer. What kind of woman does he think I am?

And why does it matter that I want him to have a good opinion of me?

He's my boss. My friend. That's reason enough.

"No," I say. "I haven't started advertising yet."

"How do you plan to find clients?" He replaces the glasses on the bridge of his nose.

"Word of mouth, hopefully."

"But how will you find the very first one?"

"Why? You want to volunteer?"

I'm joking, but the way he straightens in his seat—his gaze sweeping over me—squeezes my lungs. "Um, well. I told you there *is* a woman I've liked for a long time."

I swallow hard. It's an involuntary reaction, I swear. Purely biological. I NEED A DRINK. THAT'S IT, PEOPLE.

Gah. *Focus, Kayla.* Right. I need more information. "So why haven't you asked her out?"

His eyes wander to the kitchen door that separates us from the rest of the world. "I don't know that she sees me … like that."

I follow his gaze. Why is he looking …?

Hannah.

Of course he's talking about Hannah. The sweet Southern belle who has worked alongside him for years. She's demure and lovely and everything he could want in a woman. The perfect girl for a guy like him.

And she's the exact opposite of me.

Which makes complete sense.

"So you want to hire me?"

He looks at me again. "How much do you charge?"

"For you?" I tease, giving him my best grin. "If you'll offer yourself as my guinea pig, I only require liberal amounts of free coffee in exchange." (I get this anyway as an employee, so it's not like I'm asking for the moon.)

Something lights in Josh's eyes. "Seriously? You'll take me on as a client?"

"Of course." I point at the kitchen door. "And when I'm done with you, Hannah won't be able to refuse your charms."

"Hannah?" His voice hitches again. Maybe I've embarrassed him by guessing his dream woman's identity. But there shouldn't be secrets between coach and client.

Still, he needs to know I'll use my absolute highest level of discretion, so I lean across the table and pat his hand. "Don't worry. Your secret is safe with me."

He blinks, then nods. "When do we start?"

"Let me spend this evening making a plan for you and then we'll go from there. But maybe tomorrow night?"

"That works for me."

"Great."

As he leaves me alone in the kitchen, I pump my fist in the air. I have my first client. And sure, it's not a paying one, but it will be more than worth my time to have someone to bounce ideas off of, to see which coaching techniques go over well and which don't.

We're off to the races, folks—and I am excited in a way I never was when I worked at Jamison and Associates.

Life of happiness, you are mine for the taking.

six

. . .

SPEED DATING SHOULD HAVE its own dedicated circle of hell, like in that terrible poem I had to read in college.

Because there is absolutely nothing comfortable about sitting across from perfect stranger after perfect stranger, attempting to make inane conversation, repeating yourself a thousand and one times, and trying to decipher which participants are here to legitimately find a partner and which are here to score a one-night stand.

Which makes it the perfect place to bring Josh for this first coaching session. (I have my reasons, I promise!)

Checking my phone, I lean against the hood of my car in the parking lot of the bar hosting the Thursday night speed dating pajama party. I'd have preferred to go the more traditional speed dating route (at least it would have given me an excuse to wear my dressy clothes), but it was the only available mixer of this type tonight.

At two minutes till seven, Josh pulls up in his truck and climbs out. I half expected to see him wearing old-man striped pajamas (he seems the type), but instead he's rocking a pair of flannel pants and a white T-shirt.

Josh walks toward me and does a double take when he gets close. "I don't think I've ever seen you so casual."

I guess he's referring to the bright pink pajama pants and black tank top I'm wearing—and probably the fact that my hair is pulled back into a ponytail. Even though I prefer my dresses and heels (read: I'm more comfortable knowing I look my best at all times), I figured I'd have a better chance of blending in tonight if I wore this. "Just dressing the part."

"I like it." For a minute, he's staring at my shirt. Then Josh sticks his hands into his pockets. "That shirt is, uh …"

"I know, right?" I roll my eyes as I smooth down the front of my silky tank top, which says *This is my sexy lingerie.* "Evie bought this for me because she thinks she's funny. I've never actually worn it before tonight, but it was the only appropriate sleepwear that I have."

And I swear, the man turns as bright as one of the street lamps starting to flicker on overhead. It's way too fun to tease him (because I actually have a beloved pair of sweats and T-shirt I wear to bed), but I decide to leave him alone for the time being. "Come on, we're going to be late if we don't get in there."

He follows me as we head for the bar's entrance.

"You haven't told me exactly why we're dressed in our pajamas and going into a bar."

No, I didn't—because I was afraid he wouldn't show up if he knew what was coming.

The second we enter and he sees the speed dating sign behind a makeshift registration table that's surrounded by people, he rears back and grabs for my arm. His fingers are icy as they dig into my flesh. "Kayla, no."

"Chill out, Josh. It'll be fine."

He shakes his head, eyes wide. "I didn't sign up for … this."

Dude looks like he might seriously toss his cookies. (Where did that phrase come from, anyway? Why must cookies be demeaned in such a way, forever to be associated with barfing?)

Sighing, I pull him to the side, push him up against a wall, and place my hands on his upper arms. (And remind myself NOT to think about his biceps again.) "Josh, I need you to take a deep breath."

He complies with my demand.

"Good. Now, look at me."

Once again, he's obedient. I know I'm being harsh but he hired me to do a job, and I'm going to do it to the best of my abilities. For now, that means pushing him when he needs to be pushed.

"I knew that this would be outside of your comfort zone, but I've got to see what I'm working with here." And there's no better place than speed dating to assess his dating game than throwing him in with the sharks and seeing how well he swims (or how quickly he gets eaten).

I know I sound awful. But there's a method to my madness. "I'm not going to participate. In fact, I'll sit at the table just behind you and observe. Don't worry so much. These women will not bite." I pause. "Well, if they do, they'll get tossed out."

His lips fidget, like they *want* to smile but something is still holding them back.

I give Josh a little shake then let go of his arms. "You've got this, Josh Gregory. I believe in you." Pausing, I smile to try to ease him into this whole thing. "What are you afraid of? You talk with people all day long. This is no different."

"I'm not *afraid*, exactly. It's just … at work I'm serving people their drinks, asking them how they're doing. That's it." He pushes his glasses up. "The purpose of this event is to chat people up, to … flirt. And I'm terrible at that kind of thing."

"Because you hate talking about yourself?"

Josh frowns at me. "Maybe."

"Okay, well, for tonight, just forget that you hate it."

"Don't think it's that easy," he mumbles.

Behind us, the chatter grows louder. I glance back to find a swelling crowd, many of them women who already have drinks in their hands. They're laughing loudly and I can't help but notice that several of them have worn "pajamas" that would probably make their grandmothers faint.

Poor Josh. Maybe I shouldn't make him do this.

I shift my attention back to him. "You're a great guy,

Josh. You've got a lot to offer, and these women are going to love you. But if you really don't want to do it, I'll support that. I can find another way to figure out how to best help you."

He studies me. Then with one final exhale, he straightens and nods. "I guess I'm going to have to trust you, huh, Coach?"

"Yay!" Looping my arm through his, we march back to the registration desk and pick up his name tag.

Before we know it, the hostess (Pam, a forty-something woman with silver-blonde hair and perky boobs that could act as flotation devices if she ever found herself dropped in the middle of the ocean) claps her hands and welcomes everyone, giving us the basics about how the evening will work.

"I know we usually have the men move from woman to woman, but we're switching it up tonight, folks. Each man has an assigned seat and each woman will spend seven minutes at a table before moving on to the next in a clockwise manner." She sounds like a cheerleader on steroids. I get the sudden urge to hand the woman some pompoms. "If there is anyone you're interested in getting to know more at the end of the night, you will mark their name down. I'll do my little calculation thing and you'll find out if you have any matches."

Beside me, Josh is shifting from foot to foot. He swipes his hand across his forehead, which looks a little damp with sweat. I grab his non-sweaty hand, squeeze it, and he looks down at me. His eyes caress my face for a split second before he leaves to find his chair.

I do feel slightly like I'm abandoning him to the wolves, but I push the guilt aside. He's got this. He's not going to die, and it will make him stronger in the end.

Meanwhile, I scout out a table just behind him and to the right—close enough to hear, but not so near that I look like I'm part of the event—and settle in to watch the circus begin. The bar is fairly dim, but I can still see Josh's reactions. Waiting, I take a sip of my chardonnay.

The first woman to plop herself into the seat across from Josh looks normal enough (aka, she's fully clothed!), with short red hair and a shaky smile that makes her appear just as nervous as Josh.

The bell rings and Josh clears his throat. "I'm Josh."

"Sam."

"Hey."

"Hey."

Oh, sweet Skywalker. I take another swig of wine and look at the ceiling. This is going to be a looooong night.

"So, um, Sam … are you from here?"

"Yeah."

"Cool."

"You?"

This. Is. Torture. Apparently when thrown into an intensely awkward social situation, the man has all the conversational skills of a toddler on Benadryl. I rub my hands down my face as I listen to the two of them give one-word questions and answers back and forth for seven. whole. minutes.

Dude.

As soon as the bell rings, I hop out of my seat and

walk to his chair. He startles when I slide my half-finished wine in front of him. "Drink this. You need it."

He doesn't even argue, just downs it in one fell swoop.

I pat his shoulder. "Atta boy. Just pretend you're Han Solo and super smooth with the ladies."

"If I recall, he's kind of a jerk."

"Leia seemed to like him all right. And at least he's confident. Channel that."

The next participant approaches the now-empty seat across from Josh, looking at me with hesitation. "Um, should I …?"

"No, no. He's all yours." I turn on my heel and head back to my table, although now I'm realizing I need something new to drink. After I grab a water and glass of white wine at the bar, I slip back into my seat and zero in on Josh's conversation.

The woman he's talking to has a kind of Audrey Hepburn thing going on—a willowy figure, petite nose, doe eyes, and short brown hair that on any other woman might look boyish but on her looks classically gorgeous. She's wearing tasteful pajamas too.

And Josh is actually smiling at her, nodding, chuckling.

My stomach hardens. I never liked Audrey Hepburn. Too uppity. Too … something not nice.

Whoa, there. I have absolutely no reason to be clenching my jaw or thinking unkind thoughts about a woman I'm sure is very sweet, if her smile and gentle laughter are any indication.

This is good. Josh is starting to loosen up. If he can

get more comfortable talking with women, then he will be more confident in general, which will allow him to ask Hannah out, no problem.

My plan is working.

So why do I see spots dancing in my vision? Must be the alcohol combined with the dim lights.

Nevertheless, I feel much better when the bell rings and Josh gets a new companion—or should I say, two companions.

The younger woman looks barely legal. She tucks her mousy hair behind her ear and stares down at the table. "Um, hi. I'm Becky and this is—"

"Her mother." The older woman, with her bulky frame and even bulkier sweater, reminds me of Mrs. Doubtfire. "Cheryl."

"Oh. Hi." Josh grips the empty wine glass in front of him like it's a life preserver.

Cheryl pops a pen and tiny notebook from the breast pocket of her sweater—because OF COURSE SHE DOES. "Josh, is it?" she says as she points at his shirt, where his name tag states that he is indeed Josh. At his nodding, she writes something on the paper. "Okay, Josh, I've just got a few questions for you to start off. What do you do for a living? How much money do you make? How many lovers have you had in the last year … no, let's say two years? And if you were to date my daughter, what would your intentions be?"

The sharks are circling.

And I can't help the cackle that passes my lips. This is too good.

At the audible evidence of my glee, Josh glances back at me, wide-eyed, and mouths, "Help."

Nearly giddy with laughter, I lean forward, intent on observing exactly how he is going to handle *this* one. Dang, I really wish I had some popcorn about now.

"Excuse me."

My movie-watching vibe is completely thrown off by the voice hovering to my right.

I glance up, annoyed at the intrusion, to find Pam and her flotation devices right by my face. "What?"

"Ma'am—"

Oh no, she didn't. The woman is clearly ten years older than me, AT LEAST. *Ma'am,* my right toe. "Yes?" I say it as sweetly as possible because I just want to get back to my regularly scheduled programming, but there's still a biting edge to my question.

"You're scaring the other participants."

I must have misheard her. Maybe the wine really is going to my head. "Come again?"

"Your rather … intimidating presence has been noted by several of the female guests. It seems you're giving off a *don't-come-near-my-man* kind of vibe." She is speaking with a smile, but there's a glint of something I don't like in her eye. "I'm sorry, but you need to either participate or leave."

Uh, no. No way am I throwing myself into the ring. I'm sure Pam can be reasoned with. She looks … okay, well she looks like a Beverly Hills housewife on a power trip, but maybe I can sweet talk her all the same. I've dealt with my fair share of Pams in the courtroom.

Standing, I toss on a friendly smile and nudge Pam,

pointing at Josh and lowering my voice. "He's not my boyfriend. He's my … brother. And I'm just here to support him."

"Your brother." Obviously she doesn't believe me. And yes, I'm not normally one to lie, but I cannot abandon Josh. I also don't want to announce my identity as a dating coach. I'm not sure Pam can be trusted with that information.

"Yep. And he'll be crushed if I leave. You don't want to crush his spirit, do you, Pam?" I go for my most convincing lawyer voice. "He's so cute and sweet and innocent and just needs me here with him because he just got out of a bad relationship."

Pam's mouth twitches and for a moment, I think she's going to relent. But then she slides her eyes from him to me and a cat-like smile (I told you, cats are evil!) inches across her too-well-proportioned face (is any part of this woman natural?). "I think the way you've been looking at your brother all night is illegal in fifty states, dear."

Well, I never …

Eyes flashing, I raise my shoulders to my full height (which I admit is not that tall … where are my heels when I need them?). "Fine. You need me to participate? I'll participate." Because Josh will never forgive me if I leave him.

I feel his eyes trailing me as I follow Pam to the registration table, pay the participation fee, and write my name on a tag, which I jam onto my shirt. Then she leads me to a seat that's on the complete opposite side of the room from Josh, in front of a forty-something-year-old man with a very obvious toupee and a doughy middle. He's wearing long-sleeved pajamas covered in pictures of pi—the symbol, not the food (although I could totally go for a slice of banana cream right about now).

I feel instantly sorry for the guy, who is fidgeting in his seat like a kindergartner with ants in his pants.

"Kayla, this is Larry. Larry, Kayla." She squeezes my shoulder and gives a nice little wiggle of boobage. "I'm sure you two will hit it off just fabulously. Larry is a math professor and a regular at our events."

Oh. Math. Pi. Riiiiight.

Pam's gaze dances with delight as she leaves. If I ever meet Pam in a dark alley, she'd best watch herself.

I catch Josh's eye from across the room. They're wide with surprise.

Shrugging, I focus my attention on Larry, who is staring at me. "Hey, Larry. How's it going?"

"Um, good." He blinks. "You're very beautiful, Kayla. Did you know that?"

Pam is hovering in the wings, close enough I know she can hear us. And the little witch is laughing into her hand. Well, two can play at that game. I'll show her she can't get to me.

I place my hand on Larry's extremely hairy knuckles. "Oh Larry, stop it. You're such a sweet talker."

The tips of his ears go pink. "Oh. I think you misunderstood." He lowers his voice. "I'm not really *that kind* of guy."

My lips droop in confusion. "And what kind of guy is that?"

He slips his hand out from under mine. "I'm not here looking for a hookup."

I. Can't. Even. "I'm sorry?"

But now he won't look at me. He's just doing this strange head shaking-bobbing thing. "I'm a nice man who likes to take long walks on the beach and eat pie— get it, pie?" He points to one of the symbols on his shirt. "And I'm sorry to have to let you down like this, but I want to be with someone who wants me for me, not just my ..."

I am choking on my laughter, but I don't want to offend the guy even though he's just insulted me a thousand ways to Sunday. "Your ... what?"

He straightens in his chair. "My body," he whispers.

Oh my word. I bite my lip so hard I taste blood.

This night is going to be longer than I thought.

AFTER AN HOUR of the most hellish evening of my life, I've been paraded in front of man after man—some who are so painfully awkward, there should be a law against it, and others who are so slimy they give car salesmen a good name. All the while, I try to keep tabs on Josh, but it's difficult when I'm so far away.

Finally, it's my turn to sit across from him. The bell has rung but the woman he was just talking with is still there, and oh, poor Josh—she's crying. Like, the kind of crying where ginormous tears are streaming down her cheeks as if there's a geyser shooting off behind her eyeballs.

"I. Just. Miss. Him. So. Much. But. He. Doesn't. Want. Me. Anymore." She's heaving out every word and he's awkwardly patting her hand.

When I step up to the seat, his eyes connect with mine, and the only thing I see is relief.

I squat beside the woman. "Hey, there. I'm Kayla. Is there someone we can call for you? Someone you can go visit who will make you a cup of tea and remind you that it's all going to be okay?"

She looks up at me, blinks. "What?"

"You just seem really upset. And I'm wondering if rather than exposing yourself to all of this right now, maybe you'd be better off going home and watching a movie with a friend or something." I give her my first genuine smile of the night.

Because whatever her backstory, I have been this woman. I have given my heart to a guy and had it squashed like it didn't matter, which is why I will never do it again. But that's my choice—I know I'm happier this way. Still, it's not what this woman needs to hear right now. She needs to know that she will survive this. She needs to know that this is not the end.

"I … I guess my sister is home tonight."

"Good." I glance up at Josh, who is watching me in that secret way of his. "I'm going to help her get out of here. Want to come?"

He hops out of his seat like it's pavement in the middle of a Phoenix summer and he's barefoot. "Absolutely." Clearly he wants to escape this nightmare as much as I do.

All three of us head for the front of the bar. After I walk her to the restroom to clean the goopy mascara off her face, the woman thanks us and says she'll be all right, then slips out the door before we can argue.

Josh turns to me, hands in his pockets again. "That was really kind of you, Kayla."

"It was nothing." I wave it off, because it really wasn't more than basic kindness. Anyone else should have been willing to do the same.

"It wasn't nothing to her."

That's when I glance up, into Josh's eyes—and what I see there stills my heart. His gaze is warm, like always, but there's … more.

Admiration, maybe?

That's good. If he admires me, he'll listen to me. Thus, I'll be able to help him with Hannah.

I'm not going to read any more into it than that.

"Yes, well." I nod at the open door. "Ready?"

"I've never been more ready to leave a place in my life."

Chuckling, I turn to go. But at that moment, Pam chases us down, a smile plastered to her faker face. "Yoohoo! Where are you going? The event isn't over yet."

I turn and simper. "I'm sorry, Pammy Poo, but we've just simply been *overwhelmed* by the *delightful* company here this evening and need to go."

She narrows her eyes and places a hand on her ample chest, then glances between Josh and me, a snarl taking the place of the fake smile. "I'm so glad you and your *brother* could make it. I hope you *enjoy* the rest of your evening." A quick waggle of her eyebrows makes her implication clear as she turns on her heel and huffs away.

"Brother?"

"Ignore her." I grab hold of Josh's hand and yank him out the door into the cool evening air, gulping the freedom. "Oh my gosh, that was …"

"An experience."

A laugh bubbles in my throat. Within seconds, we are both standing on the edge of the parking lot, and I'm laughing like I haven't in ages, nearly doubled over. "You should have seen your face when Cheryl asked what your intentions were with her daughter."

The bright moon overhead is the only witness to our hysterics.

He pokes me in the side. "You looked fairly wide-eyed yourself when Mr. Pi Pajamas said whatever he did to you."

"Oh, yeah. The guy who thought I wanted to jump his bones."

"What?" Josh removes his glasses and wipes tears from the corners of his eyes. "Ugh, why did you make me do that again?"

"Because …" But I don't want to explain my reasoning to him just yet. I still need to implement the next part of my plan, and that requires keeping him in the dark. "Quick—tell me three things you would never do."

"Why?"

"Just as an exercise of sorts."

"You go first."

"Me?" I brush a strand of hair back that's come loose from my ponytail. "You're the one we're here for."

"Humor me." He kicks a pebble from the sidewalk back into the pile of landscaping rock that abuts the building.

"Fine." We start walking toward our cars as I think. "Okay. Let's go one at a time. I would never back down from a dare. Like, if someone dared me to eat fried worms smothered in butter, I'd do it."

Josh's lips twist into a grimace. "I'm not so hip on trying exotic foods—so let's call that my number one. But I admire your adventurous spirit."

"Noted." I stop in front of my Prius and lean back against the driver's side door. There's a bit of a chill in the air and I shiver. "Okay, number two. I would never allow someone to disparage my friends without speaking up and fighting for them."

"That's one of the things I really like about you, Kayla." As we stand there, Josh's words feel close, like they're hovering over me. "You're so loyal. The people in your life are really lucky to have you in their corner."

The awe in his voice leaves me momentarily breathless. I feel … exposed. Like he's uncovered a secret. Which is dumb, because yes, I *am* a loyal person. But for so long, there wasn't anyone in my life whose corner I was in. Not until Evie and my other housemates.

And now, Josh.

I'm in his corner.

Because I'm his coach, I mean. Of course, that's what I mean.

What were we talking about again? Oh, right. "Your turn." I tuck my arms across my chest.

He settles against the car beside me, and the vehicle rocks with the movement. "Number two. I'd never get up in front of people if I didn't have to."

"You hate public speaking?"

"Anything where the attention is on me, I guess. It's unnerving, and I feel like a bird being watched, waiting for someone to shoot me out of the sky at any moment."

"Stage fright. You hate being the center of attention. Got it."

He nudges me with his elbow, but there's something almost tender in it. A million invisible ants scurry up the length of my arm. *It's a chemical reaction to his touch, nothing more.* I get that, but then why does this whole night suddenly feel a lot less like work and more like two friends shooting the breeze?

Well, we are friends. That's the only reason the line is blurred.

I exhale and squint up at the stars, most of which are obscured by wisps of clouds. "Number three. I will never let a man control me."

The minute the words leave my mouth, I wish I could hit recall like you can on an email. But they're out there, in the universe, and Josh has heard them. I know it because he stiffens and turns to me. "Kayla, did someone hurt you?"

And his voice, well … I've never heard him mad

before. But that's the only way to describe the harsh harmony coating his tone.

"Not in the way you're probably thinking." I've said too much already and have absolutely no desire to hash out my past here, with him. But I can't let him think I'm a victim. Or weak. "What I mean is, I will never let a man—or the way I feel about him—dictate my actions. I am in control of my own destiny, and I'm not inviting anyone else into that space."

Because even though I'm the girl who will take any dare, I can't risk this.

"Ah."

We stand there, quiet, for what feels like an hour. Finally, I fake a yawn. "We've both got an early shift, so guess we should call it a night. Do you want to meet again tomorrow after work?"

"As long as there is no speed dating involved." His light chuckle tells me he's joking—although I'm sure if neither of us ever hears the words "speed dating" again, it'll be too soon.

"Nothing so sinister, I promise." I start to shift away from where I'm leaning, but his fingers brush my arm, stopping me.

"Wait." He pauses. "I didn't tell you my third thing yet."

Oh, right. "Okay. What is it?"

It takes him a long while to speak. "I would never go where I'm not wanted. Where I'm not invited."

It's such an odd way to phrase it, especially with what I just said, that I look up at him. And wow, I didn't realize that our bodies are nearly touching. In fact, our faces are so close that, if I wanted to, I could tip up my chin and kiss him.

But of course, I *don't* want to.

OF COURSE.

Because he's Josh, and not only is he my friend—he's also my client. And the Number One rule of being a dating coach?

Don't fall for the client.

Which means Josh Gregory is blessedly off-limits.

A very good thing, because in this moment, I have the strongest Force-like sense that he's exactly the kind of guy with the power to break my heart … if I were to ever let him too close.

seven

· · ·

I HAVE NEVER BEEN MORE grateful for my housemates than when I walk through Josh's apartment the next evening.

The living room is completely trashed, with empty pizza boxes and beer bottles scattered on the coffee table and side tables. One guy is sitting on the threadbare black couch, huge headphones completely covering his ears as he speaks into an attached microphone while playing some sort of shoot-em-up video game on the large-screen TV.

And there's a smell, like old Chinese food mixed with sweat.

I can't help but wrinkle my nose as Josh closes the door behind us.

"Sorry. I cleaned before I left this morning, but it never seems to last long." He waves at his roommate, who doesn't even notice us, then places his hand on the small of my back and directs me down the hallway.

I ignore the heat his hand gives off. "Why don't you make them clean up after themselves?"

"It's easier to just do it myself."

"You're much nicer than me. I'd be tossing their crap out into the hallway."

He laughs. "I have no doubt."

Once we've reached his room, I step away from him. One side of the space is neat and tidy, with a few *Star Wars* movie posters tastefully arranged above the twin-sized bed and a gray duvet and pillow that look cloud-like in their softness.

On the other side of the room, the dresser has obviously consumed a pile of clothing and then regurgitated sweatshirts, shorts, and underwear all over the second bed. "I'm guessing that's not yours?"

"Uh, no." His mysterious smile is on point. "I'm not a tighty-whitey kind of guy."

He says it so casually.

My inner reaction? Anything but casual—because I have to bite my tongue to keep from asking just what kind of guy he *is*. But I don't think that my brain can handle that special knowledge right now, not when our conversation from last night keeps playing on repeat. *"I would never go where I'm not wanted. Where I'm not invited."*

I know I'm overthinking it. Josh doesn't like me. He likes Hannah. And that's great. Fabulouso. A million percent a-okay.

As it should be.

"Point me in the direction of *your* clothing then." Because the whole point of coming here tonight is not to disparage his terrible housemates and their absolute cliché of a bachelor pad, but to get a look at what I'm working with wardrobe-wise. That way I can assess whether Josh needs anything new for his inevitable date with Hannah—and the plans I have for us tomorrow night—as well as if he has anything we can use to spiff up his current look.

"The left side of the closet is mine."

I'm surprised he has a walk-in, considering the apartment is fairly small, but I head on over and start flipping through the T-shirts on the left side. The smell in here is decidedly better, and I am pretty sure it's coming from his very full laundry bag, which is hanging on the rack alongside all of his clothing.

I sneak a peek at Josh. He's sitting on the edge of his bed looking at his phone—which means he is *not* looking at me. So I do what any respectable female would do in my situation.

I pull the top shirt from the bag, bury my nose in it, and inhale.

Cologne fills my nostrils and *holy TIE fighters*. How have I never noticed this scent before? Like Josh himself, it's understated, with subtle but delicious hints of sandalwood and eucalyptus. It's entirely too manly and I want to dive into a vat of it and swim around for a while. Luxuriate like it's a bubble bath. Let it tease my skin like it's teasing my senses at this very moment.

"How's it going in here?"

Eyes wide, I drop the contraband back into the bag before turning to find Josh standing in the closet doorway. Shoot. A lazy grin flickers across his face and I get the sudden urge to kiss it away. Just a tiny taste would satisfy a world of curiosity …

No, no, no. I should not be getting distracted by his scent or his smile or his eyes—those soulful blue eyes.

I've got a job to do.

When did it get so warm in here?

"Just admiring your T-shirt collection." Aaaaand I'm back to being a super cool cucumber as I select a shirt hanging from the rack and show it off. It's black with Best Uncle in the Galaxy written across it in gold *Star Wars* font, and it legitimately makes me go *ahhhh*. "You're an uncle?"

"Yeah, my sister has three kids up in Portland."

"Is that where you're from originally?"

He nods. "Moved here about five years ago when my uncle wanted to retire and needed someone he trusted to take over management."

"Do you miss home?"

"I miss my sister and nieces. And my brother-in-law is one of my best friends."

"What about your parents?"

He's quiet for a minute as he rubs his fingers along the sleeve of the shirt I'm still holding. "I love them, but there was a lot of fighting in my house growing up. I ended up retreating to my grandparents' house most days. They used to live next door before they passed."

He says it with such love in his voice, such loss, that I want to reach for him. It reminds me of how I felt when my dad left. Of how I miss my mom—not the mom she is now, but the mom she used to be. "I'm sorry."

"What about you? Any siblings?"

"No. Evie is the closest thing I've ever had to a sister."

"And your parents?"

"Divorced." I'm not ready to tell him more than that. Probably I never will be.

"Sorry."

I shrug. "It happens."

"Yeah, but that doesn't mean it isn't hard." A pause. "So where did your love of *Star Wars* come from?"

Now this I can tell him. "My dad. I broke my leg and arm in a bicycle accident when I was nine—"

"Let me guess. You were fearlessly taking a hill before crashing at the bottom."

I shrug, smile. "Bobby Jenkins told me I couldn't do it. So, naturally, I had to prove him wrong."

"Naturally. You'd never back down from a dare, right?"

"Exactly." Chuckling, I run my thumb over the white hanger in my hand. "Anyway, the accident happened at the beginning of summer and there wasn't much else to do but sit on the couch and read or watch movies, so my dad introduced me to *Star Wars*. We must have watched every film twenty times at least." I pause, a gentle smile building. "Those were some of the best months of my life."

I'd thought Dad had felt the same. And yet, six months later, he left us.

I didn't hear from him again until years later, when he showed up on our doorstep asking for another chance. I pretty much slammed the door in his face. Of course, it happened a week after Brendan kicked me to the curb, so my heart was already feeling pretty raw.

And now, if Mom's latest text about him is correct—yes, she sent another one this week—Dad is suddenly desperate to see me again. Maybe he needs a kidney. *Well, too bad, bucko. You lost your chance at free organ donations when you decided that Mom and I were too much for you to handle.*

I suck in a breath at the sudden rush of anger.

As if sensing I need a change in subject, Josh takes the shirt from me and rehangs it before plucking out a blue replacement. "I feel like you'd appreciate this one."

And just like that, we're back on track.

Filling my lungs with extra air, I peer at the shirt he's holding—and snort. It's got a picture of Darth Vader and says "Who's Your Daddy?"

"Please tell me you do *not* wear this in public."

His eyebrows waggle. "I can't lie to you."

"You need my assistance more than I thought."

"Help me, Kayla Clark. You're my only hope."

"You're hopeless, all right. Out. Now." I spin him around (ignoring the hard muscular planes of his shoulders and back under my palms … um, hi) and give him a shove, then turn back to his wardrobe and shuffle around until I find the dressier clothes stuffed in the very back. There aren't many, but I do manage to find a rather rumpled navy-blue suit with a button-up shirt and tie.

I exit the closet with the suit in hand. "Does this still fit?"

He eyes it. "No idea. Haven't worn it since my sister got married like seven years ago."

"Well, try it on." I toss it onto his bed and then lower myself beside it, scooting until I'm sitting against the wall facing him. The mattress and duvet are as soft as they look, and I find myself relaxing for the first time today.

The room has gone very quiet, and Josh is just staring at me like I've grown a second head.

"Did you hear me?" I pick up the suit hanger and wiggle it. "Try this on."

"With you in the room?"

Oh. Right. But I'm nice and cozy and really don't want to move if I don't have to. "I mean, you could leave and go to the restroom to change. Or we could be adults about it," I tease. "Just start with the shirt and jacket. When you get to the pants, I won't peek." I hold up three fingers. "Scout's honor."

He leans forward and pushes my ring finger down. "Clearly you were never a Scout."

"Maybe not, but you can still trust me." I grin and bat my eyes in an exaggerated fashion.

"Got something in your eye?" He chuckles before removing his glasses. After setting them on my lap, Josh straightens. Then before I can blink he's peeling off his shirt and COME TO MAMA, because Josh-y boy has some abs.

Where in the world have *those* been hiding?

I swallow hard. There are six—count 'em, six—and they're perfect and I kind of want to run my fingers over every. last. ridge. You know, just to make sure they're real. Because I don't know why, but I didn't expect them.

And it makes me wonder what else I don't know about this man.

Much to my shame, his torso is a magnet for my eyes, and I can't help admiring how his sides narrow and sweep inward all the way down to a slim V at his waist.

"Have mercy." I'm channeling Uncle Jesse from *Full House* as the words just slip out before I can stop them.

"What's that?" He glances up as he reaches for the button-up shirt.

"Nothing," I squeak. Then I lower my voice, even it out. "Nothing." Thank the Jedi gods that Josh's lack of eyewear means he (hopefully?) can't see the figurative drool dripping from my chin as he slips on the new shirt, popping the buttons through their holes one. at. a. time. in. slow. motion.

Gah! I'm terrible. The worst dating coach in the world, because name another who ogles her clients while they change?

Exactly.

It's just ... been too long since I've been on a date (and no, speed dating absolutely does not count). Too long since I've been good and kissed.

That has to be the reason I'm feeling *this* heated at the sight of Josh without a shirt on.

In short, I'm pathetic.

The button-up is definitely too tight on him, which means we'll need to go to the store for a new one. He holds up the sleeves. "A little help?"

With what? Oh right. The tiny buttons at the cuffs.

"Um, that's okay." Because if I get near him, I'm pretty sure my hands will decide (without my consent) to do something embarrassing.

Or worse—maybe my lips will.

I cough. "I think you need a new outfit for your date."

His date. With Hannah.

Not me.

Han. Nah.

Right. Good.

I employ the breathing I learned in yoga to make my heart steady out.

He motions to the pants. "So I don't need to try those on?"

"No!" Oh my goodness, I yelled that, didn't I? "Uh, I think we should … go. Shopping, I mean. Or to get some food. Food is good. We could eat before shopping." Oh my gosh, I sound as bumbling as Evie did before I gave her confidence lessons. What is wrong with me?

I force myself up off the bed, stumbling only a little bit.

Josh's brow is furrowed. "Are you all right?"

"Yep, great. Where do you want to go for food?"

"We could order pizza or something if you wanted. The rest of my roommates won't be back till later, and Tony won't be moving from his spot on the couch until approximately four a.m." Josh starts unbuttoning his shirt again, totally unaware of what he's doing to my insides.

The idea of being in close quarters with him—even if it's just his kitchen—is oh-so-tempting. But not smart. And I, Kayla Clark, was valedictorian of my high school class, thank you very much. So obviously, I will be intelligent about this. "I think I'd rather go out," I say with utterly false brightness.

Or you could stay here and find out what those abs feel like …

Shut your hole, Emotional Kayla. You're dead to me.

"Sure, that's fine too. There's a new Mexican place up the road I've heard good things about."

"All right. I'm just going to hit the restroom first." Before I can lose another ounce of my dignity, I retreat to the hallway and head to the tiny bathroom right next to Josh's room. Running the tap, I splash a bit of cold water on my neck, then lean over the laminate countertop and stare at myself. My green eyes are wide with something like terror. What is happening to me?

"Pull it together, sister," I hiss at the vision in the mirror. "This is your business, your livelihood now. You cannot allow emotions or dumb hormonal attraction to get in the way. Besides, he doesn't like you. He likes Hannah. The sweet girl. The adorable girl." *The girl who is easy to be with, easy to love.* "And that's not you."

Inhaling through my nose, I nod, satisfied with the pep talk.

Because if there's one thing I can't afford to forget, it's that as much as I might crave it deep down, love with a man like Josh is not in the cards for me. I cannot risk my heart, surrender my hard-won happiness, tear down my self-imposed walls—not for anyone.

My mom did that once, and look where it got her.

Look where it got *us*.

No, I'm better off alone. And I like it that way.

Sure, you do.

I lift my chin in defiance. "Control equals happiness, Kayla Clark. Don't forget it."

eight

. . .

THE GYM IS the perfect place to burn off pent-up tension of all kinds.

Specifically, the gym where Lauren's cycle class is held.

Right now, as she leads us in a series of hills, I both love and hate her—the latter because my thighs are literally shaking with exertion, but the former because she's helping me focus on something other than my time with Josh last night.

When, after leaving his apartment and before shopping for a few new outfits, we ate dinner together and he told me more about his life. He went to community college but never figured out what he wanted to do job-wise until a bad breakup (he didn't elaborate) sent him looking for a change. That's how he ended up here in San Diego, managing his uncle's coffee shop.

"Do you think you'll stay there long-term?"

"Probably. It's a good job." He paused. "I know it's not

fancy or grand, but I like being around people and serving them, making them smile. It's not a bad way to spend a life."

"That's a really nice sentiment, Josh." The scents of salsa and salt comingled in the air around us and mariachi music marched somewhere in the rafters of the restaurant. "I wish I was as altruistic as you."

"Your new business is going to help people, just in a different way."

"True, but I want to make lots and lots of money." I smirked, though there was something false in it. "Okay, fine, I also want to help people."

He averted his eyes and pushed the cheese from his enchilada around on his plate. "I definitely don't think it's bad to want monetary security. But if we're putting that above people ..." He shrugged. "I'm not sure those dreams are worth it, in the end."

His words sucker punched me, but I recovered quickly. "So what's your big dream then?"

"Mine? Nothing big about it. It's pretty simple, really. I'd like to buy my own house. I've almost got enough saved for a down payment."

"With your roommates, I don't blame you for wanting to live alone."

He smiled, contemplative. "Yeah, that's part of it. But I guess that mostly I want to live somewhere I can make into a home—where I can hopefully raise a family someday." He inhaled and peeked back up at me. "Maybe sooner than later."

And I swear my ovaries danced at the sentiment.

My ovaries do not dance, you guys. But dance they did.

Which is why I'm here at the gym, sweating like a

freaking pig (do pigs actually sweat?) in an attempt to forget. So far, I am not doing a great job because Josh's face (and fine, also THOSE ABS) keeps flashing in my brain as I spin my clipped-in heels to the beat of an 'N Sync song (because Lauren is completely obsessed with 90s boy bands).

"Argh." I increase the resistance on my bike and stand in my seat, narrowing in on Lauren, who is up front wearing a head mic. Her tight body is more muscular than mine and she's a powerhouse of pompoms and steel—both encouraging and fierce. A sorority sister and a coach, all wrapped up in one powerful package.

"Let's go, ladies. Do not slack. You've got this. I believe you can fly," she warbles that last part like the goofball she can be.

Each and every muscle in my legs burns, but I manage to focus on pedaling like my life depends on catching the next hill. Eventually, she leads us through the cool down, then stretching.

"You did so awesome today, ladies. Thanks for spending your Saturday morning with me."

Women start chattering and Lauren cuts the music. I grab my water bottle and towel, which I loop around my neck as I walk toward Lauren.

A few classmates beat me to her, young twenty-somethings who look like they could use a good meal. "Thanks for that killer workout!" One chipper blonde pulls out her phone and holds it up selfie-style while her brown-haired friend sidles up to Lauren. "Can we snap a pic with you? I want to do a shout-out about your class on Insta."

Lauren's eyes widen, because—for some reason she's never divulged to me—she hates social media. She never lets us take pictures of her unless we promise we won't post them online. "Oh, actually—"

The chick snaps the photo anyway.

Lauren's bright sweaty cheeks go pale.

Before the blonde can leave, I snatch her phone from her hands.

"Hey!"

I swipe until I find the photo and delete it. "Sorry, ladies. Our friend here is camera shy. You need to get her permission first."

"I totally did." The blonde's eyes are narrowed, but then doubt sets in.

I don't want a fight, so I grin. "How about I take a photo of you and your friend in front of your bikes?"

"Or better yet!" Lauren's frozen limbs are now working as she comes to my side and slips an arm around my sweaty shoulders. "Get a selfie with San Diego's newest dating coach."

The brunette lifts an eyebrow. "Dating coach?"

"That's right. Not that *you* need any help, but if you did want some confidence lessons or for her to help you snag the man of your dreams … well, she's the best."

The blonde studies me. "Really?"

I lift a shoulder, shrug like it's no big deal. "Yep."

"Cool. I'll bet some of my followers would be interested in something like that." She and her friend flank me and, after Lauren slips out of the way, snaps a picture of us all duck-facing the camera. "What's your handle?"

I rattle it off to her and she types something into her phone before punching the screen with her thumb and lowering her hands. "All right, you're gonna be famous now." Arm in arm with her friend, the blonde leaves.

"Thanks for intervening." Lauren bites her lip as she slips the microphone off her head. She's got another class starting in fifteen minutes, so instead of putting it away, she hangs it on her bike.

"No problem. Thanks for kicking my butt. I needed it today."

"You seemed pretty tense. Everything okay?"

I squirt a stream of water into my mouth and swallow before saying anything else. "Just stressed about the business, I guess. And my new job at the coffee shop … well, let's just say I've got the makings of the world's worst barista." As we leave the cycling space and head toward the locker rooms, I tell Lauren all about my oh-so-fun mornings at Java Awakening this week.

She giggles. "I'm sure you'll get better."

"Probably." We enter the locker room, which smells overwhelmingly like chlorine because the pool is just on the other side of one door. Women of all shapes and sizes use the benches to change, and the room echoes with their chitchat. I need to shower off before heading to work in an hour, but I've got a little time to talk before then. "Josh said he's not worried."

Once we arrive at the bank of lockers where mine is located, Lauren takes a seat on the bench nearby as I work the combination on my lock. "So, this Josh. Is he cute?"

My fingers fumble. "He's not really my type." I try my combination again, but get it wrong. What gives? I tug at the lock and curse.

"You sure about that?"

I turn to find her grinning at me. "Yeah, why?"

"I don't seem to recall the last time you were so flustered over a question. In fact, not sure I've ever seen you flustered at all." She stands, crosses her arms over her chest as she studies me. "You like him."

"No. He's my client."

"Your client?"

"Yeah, well, kind of." I explain the situation as best I can. "So, see? He likes this other woman who is totally different from me."

"That doesn't mean you can't change his mind."

"That would be unprofessional." I finally—FINALLY —get the stupid lock open and start fishing my clothing out of the purple gym bag inside. "I've got a lot riding on this and I can't afford to let some dumb attraction foil my plans."

"A ha! So you *are* attracted to him."

"No." My hands fist my clothing and toiletries bag tightly as I pull them to my chest and slam the locker door. "I mean, maybe a little, but—"

Lauren squeals and claps, ignoring the stares of the nearby gym patrons in various stages of undress. "I knew it! Girl, I can't even remember the last time you went on a date."

"Exactly. And that's my problem. It's been so long

that I am fantasizing about a guy I have no business thinking about in that way. He's not only a client—he's my boss too." I mean, he's the least boss-like boss in the history of bosses, but this sounds like a solid excuse, so I'm running with it.

"Hmm." Lauren squints at me like she's trying to puzzle something out. "What does Evie say about all of this?"

"I haven't told her yet."

"Really? I thought ya'll were as thick as thieves."

"We are, but ..." I frown. "She and Connor are so new and always together ..."

"And she's moving out soon." A knowing look comes over Lauren's face.

"She's busy."

"Yes, but you're pulling away from her before she can pull away from you, aren't you?"

And suddenly, we're in dangerous territory. Lauren and I are friends, but we've never gone deep. Not like this. And while there's something completely uncomfortable in it, I find that there's also some level of understanding in Lauren's features. Somehow, she gets me.

But I don't want to be got. Gotten. Whatever.

I want to focus on my business and get my mind off of the inevitable loss of Evie. Off of the unwanted attraction I feel toward Josh.

Off of all that and back on the things I *can* control.

"So, speaking of the dating thing ..." I nibble my lip. Because yes, this is the distraction I need. "Do you know any guys from here that you could set me up with?" There are all sorts of apps nowadays, but ain't nobody got time for that. Besides, I like to at least have one level of vetting so I don't end up on a date with a complete creep who expects sex in the restaurant bathroom just because he paid for my dinner (true story).

"I'm sure I do." Lauren tugs her ponytail holder out and shakes her hair before combing her fingers through it. Then she lifts her hair and ties it back again. "Are you positive that's what you want? Maybe you should consider throwing caution to the wind and seeing if there's anything there with this Josh guy."

No, see, Kayla Clark does not throw caution to the wind.

The wall I've built around my heart—at least as far as it concerns men—is made of bricks labeled CAUTION. Caution is my friend. Caution will not abandon me when things get too tough.

When, like my mother, I inevitably become too much for the nice guy to handle.

Shaking my head, I force a smile. "I think a blind date with a hot guy is exactly what I need right now." Because I need to get my mind off of the client I can't have and back on track.

After a few seconds, Lauren nods. "All right. Let me think about it and I'll get back to you with some options ASAP."

Good.

ASAP is good.

Especially since I have to see Josh tonight for another coaching session. And this one is going to be a doozy.

nine

"YOU WANT ME TO DO WHAT?"

Josh and I are standing at the edge of a hotel ballroom, where a wedding reception is underway. The place is gorgeous, with gauzy pink drapes lining the walls, flowered vases serving as centerpieces, and votive candles dousing the dimness in light that flickers on the wall in time to the music as couples sway on the dance floor.

"We're going to go in here and eat some food and talk with people like we belong."

Tonight, he's dressed in the new black slacks and blue button-up shirt we bought last night after dinner. His hair has been tamed with gel, although a bit still curls at the nape of his neck.

I'm sporting a black silky V-neck pantsuit that is missing most of the back and, of course, my beloved heels. (I may have stroked one and declared it "my precious" when no one was in earshot because I've missed wearing them so much.)

When Josh first saw me ten minutes ago, I thought his jaw was going to drop off his face. That did not help my resolve to stay far, far away from him, romantically speaking. For a brief moment, I considered wearing a mumu tonight—no, really, I have one that I bought for Halloween a few years ago—but knew that would make it seem like I'd been affected by Josh, like I was trying to hide. And since he is altogether too observant, I didn't want to give him any indication that I was feeling anything but normal.

"So we're crashing a wedding," he says.

The bride and groom are now leading the pack in a rousing rendition of the *Electric Slide*. "Yep." I bump my hip against Josh's. "We're going somewhere we aren't invited."

He stares at me—and it's almost a glare. Whoa, I didn't know Josh *could* glare. It's kind of like a sexy sort of smolder, a la Theo James in the *Divergent* movies …

No. Bad Kayla. It's not sexy at all.

AT. ALL.

"You're using my list against me?"

I pinch his elbow. "Not *against* you. In your favor."

"And how's that?"

"Facing your fears will help to build your confidence." I tug him inside the ballroom. We are officially wedding crashers. A tiny thrill races through me.

But unlike me, Josh is stiff, glancing around like he's expecting Storm Troopers to show up and take us into custody at any moment. "I fail to see how."

"When you're stuck in your comfort zone, sometimes you have to do something to shake things up. Right now, you don't think it's possible to ask Hannah out. But you didn't think you would ever crash a wedding, and look at you now. Once tonight is over, you'll know anything is possible."

He lets out a frustrated laugh. "You and your dating coach logic."

"You love it." Just then, a waiter passes by with a tray filled with fancy appetizers. I lift my hand. "Excuse me, could we get some of those?"

He stops, grins at me, and lowers the tray. "Anything for a pretty lady like you."

"Thank you so much." I snag two off the tray, then turn back to Josh. "Here you go."

His lip is curled at the sight of smoked salmon and caviar on crispy potatoes. "You're going to make me eat that, aren't you?"

Popping mine in my mouth, I chew and moan at the lovely flavors exploding on my tongue. "It's not like I'm asking you to eat grasshoppers. This is amazing."

"But it's not a cheeseburger or pizza." Despite his protest, he does take it from me and, eventually, takes a tiny taste. After a second or two, he makes an appreciative noise and polishes it off.

"See?" I take two waters off another tray and hand him one. "Adventure can be delicious."

"I'm beginning to see your point." He's looking at me over the edge of his goblet as he drinks, and darn it if his words don't find a target in my heart.

Does he like adventuring with me as much as I do with him?

Maybe this is how it will feel with all of my clients—once I get more. Which I will, I'm sure.

Does it feel like this with Jennifer?

Sure, Rational Kayla, stab me in the heart with your ridiculously logical questions. I loathe you.

"So what do we do now?" he asks.

I ignore the dueling Kaylas in my brain and smile. "We act like we belong."

"How does one go about doing that?" His eyes are darting to and fro, apparently watching for danger.

I can't help but smile behind my water glass. "It's all about faking it till you make it. That's how confidence starts. Just pretend like you're putting on a mask, one that lets you be anything you want to be."

He's quiet for a minute, our conversation drowned out by the clinking of cutlery against glass—the crowd's attempt to get the bride and groom to kiss. From their place on the dance floor, they laugh and comply with the request.

Then Josh says, "So, this mask. Do *you* wear one? Or does your confidence come naturally?"

My limbs grow a bit heavy at the question. It's so … I don't know. Once again, I feel like I'm an orange and Josh is trying to peel back the rind so he can separate out the sections of who I am.

I don't want to be peeled. *Shouldn't* want to be, anyway. And yet, there's something in me that does want to answer his question. "I guess I don't really know the difference anymore. And maybe that's the point, you know?"

"I'm just not sure I can be fake. Not sure I want to be." A pause. "And you shouldn't have to be either. I hope you know that you don't have to wear a mask with me, Leia."

Something cools in the air—maybe the AC has come on, maybe there's a breeze from the open doorway leading to a patio, or maybe it's something inside of me. Either way, when Josh steps closer to me, goosebumps explode all over my arms.

Maybe coming here was a mistake. Maybe I really can't maintain my professionalism where he is concerned. "I'm not sure you'd like what you see underneath." I say it as a joke, but even I can hear the slight desperation, the question, in my tone. And it's pathetic and weak and—

"You should try me sometime. I just might surprise you."

No, that's exactly the last thing in the world I should do.

Bruno Mars' *Marry Me* ends and *Sing, Sing, Sing* by Benny Goodman pops on. Squeals go up from the crowd and people start swing dancing.

And to my ever-loving shock, Josh grabs my hand. "Dance with me."

I lift my eyebrows. "Can you dance?"

"My sister made me take classes with her in high school. I got to be quite proficient."

"Hmm." Yes, this is the distraction we need. "All right."

He leads me onto the dance floor and starts busting out moves I would not have thought he knew. And thanks to my mother's insistence on putting me in dance class from a young age, I can follow his lead.

We twirl and spin in perfect harmony, adding in fun kicks and increasingly difficult spins and lifts. My head is light and so is my heart as I laugh at the ridiculous faces Josh is making, at the way our bodies and minds are so in sync. We move back to back and hook our arms, and then he's flipping me over his head and—smooth as cream—takes my hand again and pulls me back to him.

All I can say is, it's a good thing I opted for pants tonight instead of the mid-thigh cocktail dress I'd been considering.

When the song ends, Josh does a final dip and then pulls me straight back up so my hands rest on his chest. Both of us are breathing heavily, staring into each other's eyes.

Then the crowd starts clapping.

Josh blinks and looks around, the magic moment broken as he realizes that his second fear has come true —he's the center of attention. I'd been planning to take him to sing karaoke, but this wedding crashing business has fortunately resulted in him facing all three of his fears in one fell swoop.

But instead of slinking away like I thought he might, he looks back at me, lifts my hand and his together over our heads, and smiles.

And I can't help but think—he faced that last fear for me. To distract me from myself, my thoughts. He somehow sensed my mood and did something he likely knew would draw attention to himself.

But he didn't care.

Before I can fully process what all that means, the bride and groom make their way toward us. Uh oh. What happens when they realize that neither of them knows us? Before I can inch us away, Josh snags my waist and draws me to his side, then slaps the groom on the shoulder. "Hey, buddy. Congratulations again on the nuptials."

I stare at Josh, who winks at me. Uh oh. I think I've created a little fear-facing monster because who is this confident man? (And why does his sudden confidence make me lean into him more?)

The groom tilts his head, squinting, obviously trying to place Josh. But then he breaks out into a grin. "Tommy, my man!" He slurs a bit and thank goodness for copious amounts of alcohol and its ability to impair memory and make Josh look like Tommy, whoever he is. "How are you?"

"I'm great, man. And I don't need to ask how you are." He grins, extending his hand to the bride. "Nice to meet you."

"You too. I've heard so much about you, Tommy." The bride is sweet, squeezing Josh's hand. "You two were amazing on the dance floor."

"Yeah, man," says the groom. "When did you learn to dance like that?"

"Oh, here and there." Josh laughs, his fingers tickling my side with the movement. "Great party. We won't keep you."

"The DJ needs us over at the cake, anyway." The bride smiles. "Make sure to get yourself a piece once it's cut."

"We sure will." Josh wiggles his fingers. "Bye."

As soon as the bride and groom are gone, I turn into Josh and bury my face in his chest, laughing.

He chuckles into my hair. "I think you've proven your point. What do you say we get out of here?"

I pull back. "I don't know, Tommy. I think your buddy the groom would be sad if you leave now."

"True, but the mission is complete, isn't it?" Shaking his head, he lets me go—and I suddenly feel bereft.

Oh. Right.

To Josh, this was all an act. The fulfillment of an assignment—one that *I* gave.

And I'm the fool who thought for a tiny glimmer of a second that it was more.

I straighten my spine and force a smile. "Yep, and you did good, young *padawan*." I salute him and then march out of the ballroom, my heart under new guard.

Tonight was fun, sure, and that's all well and good. But I've been playing with fire and I have no desire to get burned. Lauren will come through for me and find me a date with someone who can get my mind off of … whatever this was tonight.

And I'll keep building my business, moving forward.

Soon, I'll be able to quit working at Java Awakening. Things will go back to normal.

Just the way I've planned.

ten

· · ·

TURNS OUT, I didn't need a date with a hot man to get my mind off of Josh, because the last two weeks have been insane. Even though Lauren came through and found me "the perfect guy," I haven't had a spare minute to reach out and schedule something.

It's the Saturday of Labor Day Weekend—a little more than three weeks after I decided to start my dating coach business—and thanks to that blonde chick from the gym and her post on Instagram, I've been inundated with requests for client meetings. Apparently she is some sort of influencer with a freaking ton of followers.

It's such a fluke thing, but I'm not complaining because it's meant money starting to come in—and a busy schedule.

I like busy. Busy keeps my mind engaged and my body from reacting in inappropriate ways.

It's five-thirty in the evening and I'm at a table at Java Awakening poring over my laptop as I sip an iced mocha I made myself. (Because I'm getting better—I only ruined three people's coffees this week!). I like to conduct my initial meetings in public (to make sure the client isn't a total nut job), so even though I'm off shift today, I've been here since eleven and have met with ten potential clients.

The list has ranged from an eighteen-year-old high school senior who wants to up his confidence and finally ask out the girl he's been crushing on for eleven years (so sweet!) to the eighty-three-year-old grandma who somehow got confused and thought I communed with the dead. (I honestly have no idea how she made that leap from dating coach to medium, but she was a kind woman nonetheless and we chatted about knitting and her cats for the full half-hour of our meeting.)

As soft music plays from the speakers overhead, I scan the calendar pulled up on my screen. My schedule is busting at the seams, but I need to fit my friend Jennifer in somewhere. I've finally found a man for her (one of my new clients, actually!) and she wants some help selecting an outfit and working on her confidence before the big date next weekend.

Hmm. Maybe tonight? That could work if I bump my scheduled time with Josh—he and I are supposed to grab dinner and do some coaching-slash-confidence lessons when the store closes. But I've already rescheduled on him a few times. Although I've felt bad doing it, he's been super understanding.

I'm actually not trying to avoid him. Those pesky feelings I had for him a few weeks ago? I'm chalking them up to the stress of quitting my job and him being nice to me and me just not being myself. (I promise, I'm back to normal. And no, it's not denial. It's. Not. No matter what stupid Rational Kayla may tell you.)

Of course, it helps that I have been working most of my shifts at Java Awakening with Hannah. And when Josh and I *have* worked together, it's been really busy, which means not much more than casual conversations. Thankfully, things have returned to the previously comfortable status quo between us.

A text buzzes from my phone on the table. I reach for it absently as I try to work out in my head how I can balance all the things. It's from Mom. *I've blocked your father's number but he keeps finding ways to contact me. It's getting ridiculous, Kayla. Just call the man and tell him yourself that you don't want to see him. I'm tired of being your conduit.*

I see red as I pound out my reply none too gently. *Gee, love you too, Mom. Thanks for your understanding. I mean, it's not like I haven't been building up my new dating coach business or anything. It's going well, thanks for asking.*

Three dots pop up on the screen, indicating she's writing me a message. But before it comes through, a loud laugh from behind the bar catches my attention.

I pop my head up to find the source. Hannah is standing next to Josh, who is working the espresso machine. Since it's nearly closing time on a Saturday night, the place isn't all that full. Hannah is leaning with her elbows planted back against the counter, and she's looking up at Josh, giggling. Then she slaps his arm at something he says.

My neck prickles as I watch their interaction. She's so clearly into him.

But him? He just kind of chuckles, but there's no other indication that he has the slightest interest in dating the woman.

Good grief. No wonder he hired a dating coach. The man has no flirting skills whatsoever. If he were to just act with her like he acts with me—comfortable, able to joke around (even if it's in his quiet way)—then they'd be on a date tonight instead of him spending his evening with me.

Guess that means I have my work cut out for me. It also means I can't cancel on him tonight. He needs me.

The later part of my week isn't quite as full (and I don't need to sleep, right?), so I manage to find a free spot in my schedule on Wednesday and shoot Jennifer a text before starting to pack up my laptop. With five minutes to closing, Josh is wiping down the counter when I approach. He glances up. "We still good for tonight or do you need to reschedule?"

"We're good. Do you want to go out for dinner or get takeout?"

"Whatever you want to do. It might be easier if we just get something delivered here."

I consider the options. He might feel more comfortable having his coaching session somewhere private, but we aren't going to get that at either of our places. The coffee shop seems as good a solution as any. "I'll order a pizza if that sounds good?"

"Sure."

The bell over the door jangles as a guy walks

through one minute before closing. He's dressed casually in shorts and a tight T-shirt that shows off his muscular, corded arms. His black hair is short but stylish, and his skin appears even more tan when he flashes a white smile my way. "Are you Kayla?"

Whoa. Um. "Yeah." I glance at Josh, who has his hawk eyes on the guy. "Do I know you?"

"No, but I'm friends with Lauren. She texted and said you were probably still here."

Wait. "Shane?" As in, the guy Lauren wants to set me up with?

He nods. "I know it's kind of presumptuous of me to show up like this—I could have just called—but I thought I'd have better luck persuading you to go out with me if I begged in person."

I'll admit it. The guy's smooth. Flirtatious. Fun.

Now *this* I'm familiar with. This I can work with.

I jut out my hip and flash him a saucy smile. "No begging necessary. I'd love to go out. I just need to find an open spot on my calendar."

"Well, I'm free whenever." He laughs, pushes a hand through his hair, and the action emphasizes his huge bicep. "That makes me sound desperate. I'm not, I promise. But you're gorgeous and Lauren seems to think we'd have a good time."

I pull out my phone (flicking away the notification about Mom's responding text) and squint at my calendar again. If I moved a few things around, I suppose I could squeeze him in next weekend. "How does Friday sound?"

"Aren't you working?"

I jump at Josh's voice. Oops. He's still standing right there. "Just in the morning." Smiling at Shane, I nudge my chin toward the front. "We're about to close, so I'll walk you out."

"I'll walk *you* out," he teases.

Rolling my eyes, I start heading to the door. "I'm staying. I work here."

"Right, right." He chuckles and we're at the door in seconds. "Well, Kayla Clark, I'm looking forward to our date. Until Friday, then." Leaning in, he presses a kiss to my cheek, and not gonna lie—the dude smells incredible.

"Can't wait." I open the door and he steps out.

When I turn around, I find Josh staring at me. He almost looks … pained. But that's ridiculous, because there's absolutely no reason he should.

There's also no reason I should feel guilty.

And yet, for some reason, I do.

WHILE HANNAH and Josh finish cleaning the now-empty shop, I hang out back at the table where my stuff is and put in a pizza order. By the time Hannah waves good-bye, I'm all ready for my coaching session with Josh but he's still wiping down the espresso machine.

It's a necessary part of the process at the end of every shift, don't get me wrong. The only problem? I watched him clean it meticulously ten minutes ago.

What's going on in that head of his?

Standing, I make my way over to him. "You ready for this?"

"Yeah, sure." His voice sounds so dejected that I want to wrap him in a hug—which, of course, I do not do.

"Why are you acting like your puppy just died?"

That elicits a tiny smirk, but he keeps swiping the espresso machine with a damp cloth like his life depends on it. "I don't have a puppy."

"Even worse." I poke him in the side and he visibly flinches. Man. For some reason, he's super uncomfortable with this. Getting a wardrobe update was one thing, but we're supposed to work on his "skills" tonight and possibly that is making him nervous.

Maybe talking about Hannah will help him relax. "Before we get into the nitty-gritty of the coaching session, I've got a question for you."

"Okay." So flat. So emotionless. He's not exactly cold, but his characteristic Josh-like warmth is missing.

That's okay. He doesn't need to be warm for me to help him. "I know you like Hannah, but why? What exactly are you looking for in a woman?"

It's not until the question is out that I realize it's kind of a selfish one. (And Rational Kayla, the jerk, is cackling inside my mind because she totally called it—the fact that there's still something in me that wonders if Josh and I could ever be a thing. If he could ever want *me*.)

But really, I *want* him to describe someone who is the complete opposite of me, because that will mean I can get any sort of ridiculous notion out of my head that doesn't belong there. So that, when these moments of weakness come, I can use logic and reasoning to stomp those feelings into the ground.

He sets down the rag and looks at me. "I told you how I used to go over to my grandparents' house all the time. How it was because my parents didn't have the best marriage."

Huh? Where is he going with this? "Yeah."

"Well, it's partly because my dad could never find a job he was happy with. He just kept striving, looking to strike it rich with some scheme or other. My mom couldn't get on board with it because of how it affected our finances. How it affected us. All the uncertainty, you know?" He pulls his glasses off and sets them on top of the espresso machine, then rubs the bridge of his nose. This is hard for him to talk about.

I place a hand on his arm in solidarity. Once my dad left, growing up in my house wasn't a picnic either, although I didn't have anywhere to run. I just stayed like a good soldier and weathered the storm, because what other choice did I have?

Josh glances at my hand, and for a moment, I think he's going to grab it. Instead, he snags his glasses, puts them back on, and moves toward the opposite counter where the register is.

Did I do something to offend him?

He settles against the counter, facing me. "My grandpa was an honest man who worked a simple job as a grocery store manager. Even though they didn't have much, they were so happy." A pause. "When my grandma got cancer, I watched my grandpa care for her day in and day out. It was such a picture of devotion and love."

As my heart twists at the sadness in his voice, he's staring at the ground. The corners of his mouth lift just a bit, like he's remembering something good and right. "I have this one memory …"

"Go on." Because I am one thousand percent invested in this. Objectively speaking, of course. It's amazing to me that love stories like his grandparents' have ever really existed, because my own family experience is so … not that.

"I came over after school one night, and they were sitting on the couch. Grandma was crocheting and my grandpa was massaging her feet while they watched a movie. And, I don't know. It just kind of hit me—that's what I want."

"A woman who will let you massage her feet?" I tease.

But the air is thick with the idea, which is altogether too delicious. *Stop it, Kayla. He's picturing Hannah as he talks about this.*

"No." He chuckles and the bubble breaks. I can breathe again. "Someone who is content to … I don't know. Just be with me, I guess. Someone I can build a life with."

"We have fun together, but I can't see building a life with you." And suddenly a different guy is talking to me (this one in my head) as I recall some of Brendan's words from our long-ago breakup.

Sheesh. What a time to think about *that*.

I inhale. "Lucky for you, I think Hannah is exactly that kind of girl."

His chin darts upward so he's looking at me again. "Oh?"

"Yep. And she's obviously into you. If you just asked her out, I'm positive she'd say yes."

"Really?"

"Yes, really."

"I didn't think she saw me like that." He rubs his chin.

"You're a great guy, Josh. You should give yourself more credit." All right. Time to get down to business. "The problem is that you've friend-zoned her without realizing it."

"What do you mean?"

"She was totally flirting with you earlier today and you just stood there like an emotionless droid."

His eyebrows go up and he barks a staccato laugh. "I'm sorry, how did she flirt with me?"

I approach him, putting on my best Southern belle impression. "Why, Joshy Poo, you are just too darn delightful for words." I'm pretty much killing it with my Hannah impression as I strut his way and wiggle my hips (and imagine my chest is much larger than it is). He's looking at me with big eyes full of mirth.

When I reach him, I place a hand on his shoulder and squeeze (and once again, ignore IGNORE the hard muscles under my fingertips). "And funny too. I just want to be here and revel in all this manly manliness that stands before me."

Tossing my free hand palm up on my forehead, I

pretend to swoon as I think of the cheesiest *Star Wars* line I can. "Hold me like you did by the lake on Naboo, so long ago when there was nothing but our love."

And I can't take it anymore. I lean forward and snort, and then Josh is laughing too as he grips my upper arms. "Somehow I don't quite remember that happening."

"Well, that's how it looked to me, anyway."

"You sure are something, aren't you, Leia?"

I freeze. Because darn it, we are standing really close and his hands are still on me and his voice sounds almost … wistful.

Almost like he *likes* the fact that I sure am something.

Okay, okay. I can handle this. Just gotta steer things back to the objective at hand. "Technically I just quoted Padmé, not Leia." Stepping away from Josh, I pivot and hop up onto the counter beside him. "But back to our coaching session. Did you see what you did just now? That's exactly what you need to do with Hannah. Be in the moment. Pay attention to her body language."

"Body language." His voice has gone all low and husky as he turns to face me again. "Like what?"

"Well." I swallow. (It's because I haven't had anything to drink in a while, NOT because Josh is making me nervous. I don't get nervous around men. Nope. Not me. I am *not* that girl.)

"When a woman is into you, she finds excuses to touch you. Like when Hannah slapped your arm and bent toward you. You can do the same." *That's good. Ease back into the instruction, Kayla.* "Of course, you don't want to be too handsy or you come across as a perv, but a little leaning is always recommended."

The air conditioning unit kicks on overhead, creating a whirring buzz in the kitchen. One of the fluorescent lights flickers. Finally, Josh speaks. "Lean in." He nods, but his eyes never leave mine. "Like this?" Inhaling deeply, he steps in front of me, then angles forward, placing his palms flat on the counter on either side of me.

He is so close. One more step and he'll be flush against the counter.

"Um, yes. Just like that." *Remain objective, Kayla. Don't you dare let your mind wander.*

"Then what?" he asks.

"Then, it's all about the little touches. Bumping elbows. Grabbing hands. Tiny caresses. Stuff like that."

"So, something like this?" His right thumb grazes the outside of my thigh, where the bottom of my shorts meets my bare leg.

The touch is so light, I shouldn't notice it.

And yet, I do.

Holy Force, I do—so much that I involuntarily bite the inside of my lip. "Mmm hmm." My hammering heart is making it difficult to breathe.

"Then what?" Josh studies me from behind his glasses. His eyes are mostly a light shade of blue, but this close I can see a darker tint ringing the pupil. And there's something in his gaze that makes me shiver.

Get a grip, Kayla. So he has nice eyes. Plenty of guys do. And remember—he's thinking about Hannah right now. Picturing her. You're just a stand-in.

The smart thing to do? Hop down off this counter right now, give him an A-plus on his dating coach report card, and send him on his merry little way back to the woman he really wants.

But I do the complete opposite of the smart thing. "And then, I guess, if you are both feeling it, you kiss her."

Ahem, excuse me. Just what in the galaxy are you thinking?

Shut up. I hate you, Rational Kayla.

We need to have a stern talk.

Fine … later. I can't be bothered at the moment.

Gah, what is happening to me? I feel more than a little outside of the control I wear like a badge. It's like something I've never felt before is curling through me, taking over every logical neuron in my brain. Like some kind of anticipation, painful and prickly, but also … exquisite.

Painful because it's breaking down that wall I've so cautiously built brick by brick.

Exquisite because there's something about the way Josh is looking at me, considering me, like I'm a fine piece of art he's not quite sure how to approach. Like he doesn't want to break me.

Doesn't he know I'm tough? Some might even say I'm made of stone.

I *usually* am, anyway.

In this moment, though? I'm glass, and the mounting tension between us is causing hairline fractions along the surface of who I am.

What is this strange effect Josh has on me?

He licks his lips, and the tiny action shoots my whole body through with heat. "Kiss her. Right. But how do I know if she's feeling it too?"

Hating myself, I slide my arms around his neck. "She might do something like this to show you."

In reaction, he takes one final step toward me, closing the gap between us. Our faces are even with each other, only inches apart.

My heart—treacherous thing!—honest to goodness skips a beat.

"Then?" His breath is warm against my cheek.

Oh, for Pete's sake. I can't take this anymore. "What do you mean *then*? You kiss her. You can't make her wait *too* long or you'll lose your opportunity."

And there he goes, brushing my thigh again, making my whole body seize with fire. "Maybe she needs to have a little patience."

And I can't decide if I'm annoyed or amused at his reply. Possibly both. "Patience is overrated."

"Noted." Josh pushes a strand of hair away from my face, tucking it back. His finger strokes the length of my ear and I'm about to have a freaking heart attack at the barest of touches. "Are you really sure about this, Leia?"

Am I?

No.

But the vulnerability in his question, in his voice, means I need to have enough confidence for the both of us. So I let go of his neck with one hand, lift the glasses off of his face, and set them on the counter beside me. Then, I push my fingers through his hair and tug him close once more. "I'm the coach, aren't I? Of course I'm sure."

Lies, lies, you sit on a throne of liiiiies.

Then—three, two, one—he leans in. His lips at long last cover mine, and there is something so achingly sweet and tender in his kiss. Josh's mouth is careful in its exploration. Slow. Almost tentative.

Then one of his hands loops around my waist and he deepens our connection to the tiniest degree. In response, my veins become a raging river of fire and I arch my back, pulling him nearer.

I'm a greedy woman, because I want more. More of his lips moving in time to my own. More of his hands pressed along my spine. More of his solid chest beneath my fingers.

More of Josh Gregory.

Suddenly there's a pounding on the front door. Josh startles at the sound and breaks away from me. I nearly fall off the counter, but manage to steady myself before hopping to the ground and glancing at the front door.

There's knocking again. "Hello? Pizza's here!"

Josh curses under his breath. "Perfect timing."

My eyes dart to his. I can't read him—he's standing there, stiff, his hand massaging the back of his neck. And his cheeks are red, like an inferno.

If the warmth burning mine is any indication, we're a matching pair.

Because now, as reality sets in, I can't believe I've crossed this line with a client—with a friend—because I enjoyed that kiss waaaaaay too much.

The kiss that wasn't meant for me.

"Sorry. Um." I can't think. "I'm not very hungry anymore. And I've got … stuff."

I need to leave now, before I throw myself at him again or do something even more embarrassing.

I'll text him later about continuing his lessons—although maybe after this, he'll decide they're not worth it. Because even the densest man in the world would be able to feel this tension between us. It's so thick that not even a light saber could slice through it.

Josh trusted me and I failed him.

I failed myself.

Before Josh can say a word, I grab my purse and hustle out of Java Awakening, past the super confused pizza delivery guy.

I've got to find a way to forget that kiss ever happened. From now on, I'm giving Rational Kayla permission to hog-tie Emotional Kayla if she must.

Because if I don't, I'm going to lose everything.

Including my heart.

eleven

· · ·

MY DATE with Shane can't come soon enough.

Because I just lived through the most awkward week of my life working at Java Awakening with Josh. He did eventually ask if we were okay and apologized if our "role-playing" got out of hand. See? He even used the term I originally did when describing what a dating coach does. To him, that's all it was. Pretending. So of course I said we were fine and that I thought he was ready to ask Hannah out on a date.

He said he wasn't sure. He felt like he could benefit from at least one more coaching session—whenever I could fit him into my schedule.

So far, I haven't been able to.

Though, I admit, I haven't exactly tried.

But tonight—tonight will help. I'm going out with an attractive man. I'm going to have drinks with him. I'm going to have fun with him.

And, if at the end of the night, he's not too big of a jerk, I'm going to kiss him.

Because I've gotta scrub that memory of kissing Josh right outta my stupid brain.

It's a brilliant plan.

Then why do I feel sick to my stomach as I pull open the door to find Shane on my porch? He's even handsomer than I remember, this time dressed in a crisp suit, and his cologne smells like patchouli—sweet and spicy and heady.

In a word? He's perfect.

Exactly what I need.

Shane whistles. "Hey there, gorgeous."

I do in fact feel gorgeous in my deep purple cocktail dress with its off-the-shoulder straps and sweetheart neckline, so I laugh and let him kiss my cheek. "You're not looking so bad yourself."

He offers me his arm. "You ready?"

"Yep." I grab my clutch and call goodbye to Alexis, the only one of my housemates who is home from work yet, and we head to Shane's car, a black Corvette. "I like your ride."

"Thanks. Tina has seen me through a lot in the last year."

What is it with guys naming their cars? We both duck inside and he starts the engine, which purrs like a tabby with catnip. Shane strokes the dashboard. "That's right, baby. Good girl."

"Should I leave you and Tina to this date by yourselves?" I tease.

"No way. She doesn't mind being the third wheel. And the fourth, fifth, and sixth as well."

Groaning, I push on his upper arm. "You didn't just say that."

He snags my hand and secures it against his thigh as he grins at me. "Oh, but I did."

With a wink, he takes off down the driveway, both of us laughing, and heads out of Point Loma toward downtown. My hand feels nice in his and there's a bit of the familiar tingle. The possibility of something new, something exciting.

And definitely something distracting.

As we drive, we chat about our jobs and hobbies. He's a hedge fund manager for a nationwide investment banking firm, and while he does enjoy Cross Fit, he's also into brewing beer, Frisbee Golf, and traveling to lots of foreign countries.

Other than the last one, which I haven't had much opportunity to do because Miranda kept me chained to a desk for seven years, we don't have much in common interest-wise. But I like his light, fun energy regardless.

When I tell him I'm a dating coach, he arches an eyebrow. "Is there a lot of money in that?"

"I'm just getting started. But yes, you can make a success of your business—if you're good at what you do."

"Are you good at what you do?" His voice teases me and he's got this sexy dimple in his right cheek that's quite diverting. I definitely made the right call in coming tonight.

"A dating coach teaches others how to have confidence, how to flirt, and how to kiss. And in order to teach those things, she's got to be good at them herself." I say all of this with a straight face.

He sneaks a glance at me. "And are you?"

I lean in. "Guess you'll have to let me know later."

Grinning, he revs the engine down the freeway. "I look forward to doing just that."

For the rest of the drive, we tease and flirt until he pulls up to a fancy steak restaurant on the bay. He tosses the keys to the valet and warns him not to dent or scratch it. Then Shane turns to me and presses his hand into my lower back, and an unbidden memory flashes in my mind—of Josh doing the same thing in his apartment hallway three or so weeks ago.

No, no, no. Thoughts of him are not allowed right now, especially memories of that night (the one in which I first became acquainted with the look-but-don't-touch wonder that is Josh's six-pack).

The restaurant is beautiful—with crystal vases and candlesticks, dimly lit chandeliers, and plush red carpets—and something smells amazing, like a combo of peppercorn and butter with a lingering hint of lemon. Shane tells the hostess we have a reservation and she gathers two menus and leads us to one of the round booths nestled into a dark corner, telling us to enjoy (though she's looking at Shane like *he's* the steak … not that I can blame her).

Because the booth is a semi-circle, we end up sitting next to each other. But rather than taking the opportunity to feel me up like some guys might, Shane is a perfect gentleman as we look over the menus, order some wine and our entrees, and settle in to wait for our food to arrive.

He entertains me with horror stories from the hedge-fund world, and he laughs at all the right times when I give him some stories in return. Something holds me back from telling the same stories I swapped with Josh that night we sat in Java Awakening after hours, though. It makes no sense, but it feels like I'm cheating on him somehow.

Which you can't really do since YOU'RE NOT TOGETHER.

Since you don't WANT to be together.

Right. Duh. I down a swallow of wine—a large one —and warmth sweeps through my veins, relaxing me. "So, where do you see yourself in five years? Or ten?"

"Well, I don't know about five years or even ten exactly, but I'd love to eventually get the senior VP slot at my firm or another similar firm. I'm willing to move just about anywhere. Definitely would love to stay in a big city, though. New York would be pretty sweet, maybe L.A."

Our steaks arrive and I cut into mine. When I raise it to my lips, I can't hold back the groan. It literally melts in my mouth.

When I open my eyes (because yeah, apparently I closed them upon the rapturous experience of tasting my food), I find Shane grinning at me. I toss on a smile and move the conversation along. "So you don't want to stay in San Diego?"

"Nah. I mean, I will if that's where I can get a job, but I'm open to wherever."

That's one big zero in the Shane column.

Wait. Not that I have columns—I don't! Because I'm not actually comparing him to Josh. How can I? Josh is not a contender in the fight for Kayla's heart. Come to think of it, Shane isn't either, because I'm fairly certain from the things he's said and the way he's said them that he's all about the fun and not so much about the commitment.

Maybe I should test that theory though. You know. For scientific research purposes. To see if I've still got it when it comes to reading guys.

I run a fork through my baked potato, where butter pools in the center. "Where do you see a wife and kids fitting into that kind of life? Wouldn't you have to work a ton of hours?"

He goes a little pale and chuckles before taking a fast swig of his own wine. "I mean, yeah, that comes with the territory. I'd be able to provide well for a wife and kids, so of course I want them. Someday." Shane tugs at the collar of his shirt, his chuckle garbled. "But I've got a long road ahead before I'm ready to even think about that. I want to be firmly established on my career path before getting married."

"I totally get that." And I do. In fact, before now, I never would have even considered dating a guy who wasn't light-years away from wanting to be married, because I have never intended to marry.

But then there were the dancing ovaries …

"I want to live somewhere I can make into a home—where

I can hopefully raise a family someday. Maybe sooner than later."

Darn Josh and his stupid romantic ideals.

Shane's shoulders visibly relax at my response. As we finish off our dinner and then a fantastic creme brûlée for dessert, we keep things light and playful between us. He pays the hefty tab without a blink and we slip outside to take a walk down by the water. Boats bob in the harbor as the fading sunlight casts its final sparkles across the surface of the bay. A chill in the air has Shane offering me his coat, and he takes my hand as we walk.

It's perfectly pleasant.

Exactly what I wanted tonight to be.

And yet, I find my mind wandering. (And, sorry to say, if you can't guess WHO it keeps wandering to, then you're dumber than a drunk Ewok.)

We stop to look at a yacht that's particularly impressive and Shane tells me that someday, he plans to own something just like it. "That's my big dream, I think."

"Why is that?" Maybe he wants to ride off into the sunset with the woman he will one day marry, enjoying her company and making their own memories under the moonlight.

Okay, seriously. Who am I and what happened to the old Kayla Clark—the one who did not wax poetic? I think I've been replaced with Evie's shorter, brasher twin sister or maybe a heroine out of one of the romance novels her publishing company puts out. Sheesh.

"I don't know," Shane says. "Wouldn't it be

awesome to have something that everyone else is jealous of?"

I laugh, because of course that's his answer. But he is exactly the kind of man I asked for, isn't he? Sighing, I lean against the wooden perch that divides the walkway from the water below. Shane doesn't seem to notice my confusion or despondency and launches into a narrative about all of his dream yacht's bells and whistles. "And there would be an eighty-inch television in the bedroom—"

"What would you be watching on it?" I don't know where the question comes from, but it's out now.

He scratches his clean-shaven jaw then shrugs. "I'm not all that particular so long as there are guns and fast cars. What about you?" Then Shane slips his arm around my waist and pulls me closer. "What's your favorite movie? *Pretty Woman*? That sounds right up your alley."

(Uh, has he actually seen that movie? If so, is he comparing me to a hooker?) Regardless, I get the sudden urge to tell him the truth—to reveal a little bit of something real about myself. Because all night long, we've been flirting and I've kept things entirely surface level. And maybe my favorite movie isn't exactly a soul revelation, but it's something that exactly two people on the planet actually know about me (fine, three if you count my dad, which I absolutely do not).

"No." I bite my lip and look up into his brown eyes. *"The Empire Strikes Back."*

"As in, *Star Wars*?" He laughs, hard. "Right, and I'm into romantic comedies. Come on, for real."

"That is for real."

"Fine, you don't want to tell me, huh?" He waggles his eyebrows. "I like a girl who keeps a few secrets."

"I just told you my secret. I am a thousand percent serious."

Shane scoffs playfully and tickles my sides just a tad. "As if a girl like you would be into that nerdy stuff."

We're just gonna pretend he didn't call me a *girl*—because I'm all woman, baby, and I really hope he knows the difference. I quirk an eyebrow. "A girl like me?"

"Smart, beautiful." He reaches up and trails his thumb across my jaw. "Sophisticated."

"And what exactly does a sophisticated 'girl' like?" I'm not really bantering anymore, but he's obviously not getting the memo. And it's not his fault. He thought I was something different than I am—and I was.

Before.

Now I'm this strange in-between Kayla. I'm not really sure who she is, but she's trying desperately to cling to the old, the familiar, the things she can control and understand.

Which is why I don't pull away when Shane leans in closer. "How about you tell me *exactly* what you like?" Then he kisses me, and I'll admit it—Shane the Blind Date is a good kisser.

Even though I'm annoyed with him, I tell myself to stop thinking and just go with it. Because that's the whole point of this date, isn't it? To remind myself that THIS is what I want? That fun and flirtation are as far as I'm willing to go?

That I have no desire to get my heart involved, because there is only trouble waiting at the end of that road?

But as Shane moves his lips against mine, I come to a startling realization.

I feel nothing. No tingle in my toes. No zipping heat. Nada. There was more authenticity in my pretend kiss with Josh than in this real one with Shane. Maybe it's the guy.

Or maybe it's me.

I jerk away from Shane and place my hands on his chest. "Stop."

"What?" He looks dazed. *I totally understand the feeling, buddy.* "Sorry, I thought you wanted that."

"I did."

But not anymore.

Now, I want inside *Star Wars* jokes and eucalyptus. I want a man who will make me coffee when I'm having a bad day (even though I can make it for myself). I want someone who will sit on the couch and rub my feet as we watch a movie.

Josh Gregory has ruined me for anything less.

"So what's the problem?"

The problem? Oh, just a tiny little thing.

The guy who has apparently become the standard I will hold all other guys to from now on? The one whose kiss I can't get out of my head, much as I try? The guy whose quiet, patient manner has traced a hot trail of desire through every nerve in my body without me even realizing it?

Yeah. He doesn't think of me in the same way.

And while I'm not the kind of woman to sit back when I want something, this is different. I won't force myself on Josh, because he's in love with someone else.

A girl who is nothing like me.

"I'm sorry. I just … I have a headache." Or a heartache. Gah. "Would you mind taking me home now?"

twelve

. . .

DO you know how creepy it is to sleep with Colin Firth's ginormous floating head staring at you from across the room, where he's positioned over your room-mate's bed?

Of course, don't even try telling Evie that. The woman loves the *Pride & Prejudice* star with a zeal that is equally hilarious and frightening. I think she might challenge me to a duel if I were to tell her the guy isn't all that handsome. Don't mess with Evie and her Mr. Darcy.

But I digress.

Saturday morning, I wake up with the stalker-y vibe that someone is watching me, and I just know it's that Darcy dude. But when I toss the covers back, I discover Evie sitting on the edge of her bed in the dark, her eyes fixed on me, one mug clutched in each hand.

"You trying to freak me out there, Evs?" I sit up and rub my eyes.

"Sorry." She holds up one of the cups. "Just wanted to say hi before I head over to the house for the day. Thought I'd try to bring you to life with some java." Her eyes squint. "Did you wear a dress to bed?"

Glancing down at my body, I wince. Oh yeah. I came straight home from my date with Shane and fell into bed without removing my makeup, brushing my teeth, or putting on pajamas. "Yeah, um, late night."

Not really. I think Shane dropped me off around ten.

Evie arches an eyebrow and sets my mug on the nightstand between our beds. "How was your date?" Then she turns and pops open a curtain, letting in a stream of morning light.

Like a vampire, I wail and duck back under the comforter.

My best friend laughs in that gentle way of hers. "Come on, Kay. I only have thirty minutes before Connor picks me up. And don't you have to work today?"

"Yes," I mumble. Don't remind me. "But not for an hour. Let me sleeeeep."

"We haven't talked in forever. You've been really busy, and that's awesome, but …"

I know that tone. Sighing, I muster all of my strength and face the light again. "But what?" I snag the cup of coffee and inhale the hazelnut scent.

"I don't know. I miss you."

"I miss you too." I nudge my chin toward Evie's boxes in the corner of our room—the ones already half-filled with her things. When I saw them last night, it was the emotional equivalent of getting kicked in the teeth right after spending thousands on dental work. "Looks like you're getting closer to the big day." Despite my mood, the coffee goes down smooth as I sip.

She bounces on the edge of the bed, unable to contain her giddiness. And she *should* be giddy. This is huge for her. "I think I'll be able to move next weekend."

That soon? The brew I just ingested gurgles in my stomach. "That's great."

"It is great." She sets her own mug down and then flops back onto her bed, sighing. "And Connor is great. Life is great."

"I'm happy for you." And I am, even if it means I'm losing her. "You deserve it."

Her head pops up. "So, what about you? How is it working at Java? How's the business going?" She pauses and gets a sly look on her face. "How's Josh?"

"He's fine." With that, I'm off the bed and leaving my mug on my dresser, flying into my closet faster than you can say "May the Force be with you."

"Oh my goodness. Kayla Clark."

"What?" I snag my silky robe off of a hanger. When I emerge from the closet, Evie's eyes are zeroed in on me.

"You like him."

I sigh. I guess there's no sense in denying it. She's my best friend and apparently can read me like a book (which makes sense, because she's an editor—ha!).

"It doesn't matter." I wiggle out of my dress from last night, fumbling for a second with the side zipper. "He likes Hannah. And even if he didn't, it would never work between us."

"Why not?"

The dress drops to the ground with a swoosh. "Because I'm me and he's him."

Evie crosses her arms. "I think I'm gonna need more information than that."

My head is starting to ache from all my tossing and turning last night, and I really don't feel like diving in deep this morning. So I give her the easy answer. "I'm just too much for a nice guy like Josh to handle."

"Well, that's the fattest load of bunkum I've ever heard—and you know it."

"Bunkum?" I can't help but smirk at my bestie's ridiculous vocabulary.

"Nonsense. Malarkey. Baloney." She screws up her face into a glare that is so comical I have to laugh.

"What are you doing with your face there?"

"I'm attempting to put on your lawyer look."

I unclasp my strapless bra, peel it off, and tug on my robe. I've got to shower, but obviously Evie is determined to have this out now. "My what?"

"You know. The face you make when you're telling me what's what and I'd better listen or else." She attempts a scowl-like thing but it comes off as a grimace. "That face."

"You just look constipated."

She deflates. "I know. I don't do it as well as you."

"It was a good faith effort."

"I still stand by what I said, though. Why do you think you're too much for him?"

"He's like the sweetest guy in the world. Patient. Good. Kind."

"Not to mention cute."

"Not just cute. He's hot." Evie's eyes go wide at my assessment, but it's the truth. "He's got abs for days, Evie. And they're glorious."

"I'm sorry, exactly *why* have you seen his abs?"

Oh, fine. I check my clock, determine I have time, and sink onto the bed next to her before telling her everything about the last month.

By the end, she's fanning herself. "All of that sounds steamier than some of the novels I edit. I fail to see the issue here. Why are you not doing that Kayla thing where you march up to him and demand he date you?"

I swat her, smacking her boobs on accident (but thankfully not hard). "I don't do that!"

"Not in so many words. But your confidence just wraps around people and convinces them to do your bidding."

"Whatever!"

She pokes me and we both laugh. "Seriously, though. Why are you settling for guys like Shane when there is a Josh around? And don't give me that stuff about you being too much. Maybe you're a lot, but that's not a bad thing. More of Kayla is a very good thing in my opinion."

"I love your faith in me." I stare up at the ceiling. "I don't know. I just understand the Shanes of the world. They don't expect much from me. A little fun, maybe. Flirtation. Kissing. But Josh … he's real." I swallow and lower my voice. "Being with him would require my whole heart."

And there it is. The truth on a platter, out for the world—for me—to see.

"That is generally how love works, you know."

"I know, but …" My eyes burn. Oh great. I grab a fistful of the comforter underneath me. "I've seen love at work. Seen what it does. It nearly destroyed my mom when my dad left. She changed. I mean, her being who she was, we were never as tight as your family, but after dad, she got a lot colder, a lot more distant. Losing love broke her open and spilled her out. And I just can't let that happen to me."

"Aw, Kay." She puts her arm around my shoulders. "There are no guarantees with love. Even with Connor, I sometimes fear he'll wake up one day and remember all the hot women he used to date and think I don't compare."

Her vulnerability has always astounded me. How does she share her heart so easily, like it's nothing to be totally open and honest? I squeeze her hand. "That's not going to happen."

"It might." She shrugs. "I don't think it will, but anything is possible. And that's scary, but it's also kind of freeing." Evie is quiet for a minute before moving on. "I know you like to control everything, Kay, but even *you* can't think up every possible scenario that might happen for the rest of your years on earth."

"I can try."

"Friend, I know you like to think you're Super-woman, but you aren't God."

"Ouch." I shake her knee. "You're supposed to be the nice one."

She laughs at my antics. "I *am* being nice. I'm telling you the truth."

"I don't want the truth. I want you to stroke my ego and tell me that I am awesome and amazing just the way I am and that I never need to change." I'm using my teasing voice, but some part of me is actually rather serious. Because the truth is hard to hear.

"You *are* awesome and amazing just the way you are." Evie lays her head on my shoulder. "And the right guy won't think you're too much or too little. You'll be just right for him. For each other." Evie grabs my hand, squeezes. "To be honest, I think Josh might be that guy. I've always thought he liked you. And that kiss … I don't know. It doesn't sound like the kiss of someone who was practicing for another woman."

Could she be right?

The thought is electrifying.

The thought is terrifying.

Because if Josh actually likes me, and if he actually were to ever do something about it, then I'd be forced to make a choice—to stay content with the Shanes of the world, or to let myself fall, praying that I won't regret it.

I sigh. "I'm really going to miss you when you're gone, you know."

"I'm just moving a few blocks away."

"It won't be the same."

"I know." Evie sniffles and I almost envy her tears. Crying is another thing that comes easily for her. Her phone buzzes beside her, and she sits up to look at it. "Connor's here."

"Okay."

"Kayla, I may be moving out, but I'm not leaving, all right? I'm not going to duck out of your life just because it takes a little more effort to spend time together." She pauses, inhales a shaky breath. "I'm not your dad. And if you give Josh a chance, I don't think he would be either."

Ah, sheesh. Her words … they both comfort and sting.

There's still a problem, though. "What if he really does love Hannah?"

"Did he ever *say* he loved her?"

"No."

"So maybe it's just a crush." She pokes my leg. "Or *maybe* he's changed his mind and likes you now."

My heart really likes that idea. But … "And if not? I don't want to be that girl who interferes with love."

"So come up with a way to tell for sure. You're so good at reading people—it's your superpower. I'm guessing if you lower your own walls and really look with an objective eye, you'll be able to tell if Josh likes you."

"You have more faith in my abilities than I do."

"That's because I'm your best friend and I can see things you don't, just like you do for me." She kisses my cheek and hops up. "Love you."

"Love you too."

LESS THAN AN HOUR LATER, I'm on my way to work, thinking about all the things Evie and I talked about. When I'm almost to Java Awakening, my phone buzzes. I connect via the car's Bluetooth system. "Hello?"

"Kayla? Hey, it's Jennifer!"

I flip on my blinker to change lanes. "Long time, no talk! How was the big date last night with Derek?"

"I'm pretty sure he's my soulmate."

Laughing, I exit the freeway. "I thought you two would hit it off."

"We totally did! He took me on a dinner cruise and then for a walk on the beach. And you know what you said about nice guys being sexy *and* good kissers?"

I tingle to remember—because I had no idea I was talking about Josh at the time. "Um, yeah?"

"Well … you were right."

"Woohoo! Get it, girl." Then we're both laughing as I'm pulling into the Java Awakening parking lot. "So I take it you'll be seeing him again?"

"For sure. And hey, listen, I wanted to ask you something. Do you have time? Sounds like you're in the car."

"I just pulled up to work, but I can stay on for a minute or two." I turn off the car and lift the phone to my ear. Outside, I see Josh pull up in his rusty blue truck. He climbs out and stretches. The bottom of his tight Henley lifts just a tad and I see a flash of skin.

Maybe I should turn my car back on and blast the AC.

Dang it. I've got it bad.

Jennifer continues. "So, my brother Lawrence lives in

New York, but he's going to be in Los Angeles soon to work on a movie he's producing."

Where is she going with this? "Okay …?"

"He is so great at his job, but he's actually really shy when it comes to women. Kind of becomes a bumbling idiot once he steps from work mode to flirt mode. I've tried multiple times to set him up with friends of mine and they all say the second he's on their date, he fails epically."

I laugh at her description. "All right. So …"

"So, if I got you a meeting with him while he's in L.A., would you work with him?"

"Oh. Well …" I bite my lip. I haven't thought about expanding the business. But I wouldn't turn down the family member of a friend, even if he lived elsewhere. We could always do our coaching sessions online. "I mean, yeah, I'd work with him if he wanted to hire me."

Jennifer squeals and I pull the phone away from my ear for a second until she quiets down. "That is so fab. He's got a ton of connections in celebrity and moviemaking circles, so if you can manage to reform him, I think he'd be happy to throw more clients your way."

"Seriously? That would be … amazing." More than I even thought to dream for my little business this soon. "Dating coach to the stars—can you imagine?"

"I know, right? Okay, I'm going to talk with him and get something on the books for you. Text me your availability."

"Whenever it is, I'll make it work." For a chance like

this? I might even sell an organ. Kidding. (Kind of.) "Thanks for making this happen, Jen."

"Are you joking? Thank you! I'll be sure to invite you when Derek and I get married." She giggles, so I know she's joking. But there's something kind of cool about the thought that I might actually have a hand in people's happily ever afters.

Like Josh said … I *am* helping people.

I hang up with Jennifer and head inside, where Josh is already opening up the register and getting the machines prepped. "Morning," I call.

He pulls the beanie off his head and runs his hand through his hair, which is getting to be on the longer side and actually kind of wavy. "Important phone call?"

"Yes, actually." As we pull the pastries Linda made from the kitchen into the case up front, I tell him about my call with Jennifer.

"Congrats. You're really doing it. I'm proud of you, Leia." Then he frowns. "I guess that means you're going to be so busy soon that you won't need this job anymore, huh?"

"Oh." I hadn't thought about that. "That's true, I suppose. But you can't get rid of me that easily. I'll still be in here all the time, just as a customer again."

His smile is soft—but do I detect a hint of hesitation in it? "Glad to hear you won't forget about all the little people who helped you make it to the top."

He's teasing, I know, but I think he might also need my reassurances, whether he likes me as more than a friend or not. I place my hand on his arm and prepare to say some of the truest words I've ever spoken. "Josh Gregory, I could never forget about you."

He just stares at me for a minute, swallows, then nods. But before he can speak, we get our first customer of the day and then it's off to the races as we serve, serve, serve.

A few hours into our shift, I glance up from the espresso machine to find Josh watching me. "What?"

"Nothing." He ducks his head, frowns, then looks at me again.

The rest of our shift is more of the same. As I'm making an iced caramel macchiato with fifteen pumps of vanilla syrup, heavy whipping cream, and extra caramel drizzle (yes, that is a real order—blech), I consider Evie's words from this morning: *You're so good at reading people—it's your superpower. I'm guessing if you lower your own walls and really look with an objective eye, you'll be able to tell if Josh likes you.*

Okay, be objective. If I saw any other guy shooting glances at any other woman, I'd think he was into her.

So maybe …

But what if I'm wrong?

Then an idea comes, swift and strong and oh so perfect. I can test this potential theory of mine, give it a chance to bloom, just like Evie said.

That is, *if* I can step past my fears, give Josh a chance to prove he is different than Brendan—different than my dad.

You are not a fearful person, Kayla. Get over this hump and who knows what your life could look like. And if your heart gets broken, well, then you'll pick yourself up and dust yourself off—and you can still go on to be a success and get that dog to cuddle with at night.

For once, Rational Kayla is coming through for me, and I kind of want to give her a big ole hug.

Taking hold of the shot of espresso I just made, I toss it into the drink I'm making, add the other crap that's sure to put the girl who ordered it into a sugar coma, and slide it across the counter to her. Then I turn and march up to Josh, who is cleaning out a blender at the sink. "I have another dating assignment for you."

He freezes, arches an eyebrow. "I thought you said I didn't need any more help."

"Just one more assignment. Then we'll be done with this little arrangement we have."

And hopefully, creating a new one—one that will have me finding plenty of ways to put that "practice" kiss to shame …

Don't get so ahead of yourself there.

Right.

"Okay." Shifting his glasses up his nose, he sticks the washed blender onto the drying rack. "What's the assignment?"

And here it is—the plan that could completely fall apart at my feet. Or the one that could change everything. "You have to execute the perfect date."

Josh's nose wrinkles. "How will you know if I complete the assignment? Are you going to tag along?"

The suggestion makes me want to shudder, slicing me through. But I manage to hold it together. "I'm not talking about your date with Hannah. I'm talking about a trial run."

"I don't follow."

This sounded a lot better in my head. "You'll plan the date but take me instead of Hannah. How does Monday sound? Is that enough time to plan?" I know I'm tossing out questions like a drill sergeant, but I'm afraid to stop and take a breath. Afraid to hear his answer.

Afraid he'll see right through me straight to the heart that's about to beat out of my chest.

But then he swallows, nods really slow. "Yeah, Monday works."

"Good. It's a date," I wink and tease, because that's exactly how I'd normally react.

But on the inside, I'm losing my flipping cool.

thirteen

I'VE BEEN on a lot of first dates.

Most guys, like Shane, go the dinner-at-a-fancy-restaurant route. The safe route. Some guys take it one step further and tack on dancing or a movie, maybe a concert or art show.

Once I had a date try to take me parasailing. That would have been fun—if he hadn't face planted in the sand during his turn and been so embarrassed that he unclipped and hightailed it out of there, leaving me stranded on the beach. (Yeah, he was a real winner.)

But I'm not sure I've ever been as surprised by a first date—or felt as comfortable—as I do right now, at the top of a beach bluff next to Josh. He picked me up around two this afternoon, and we drove in his truck (which, despite its old age, is actually very cozy) a ways out of town to a hiking route along the coast. I'd never heard of it and he laughed in that quiet way of his, saying that was kind of the point. Less notoriety equals less of a crowd.

We've spent the last few hours hiking. I'm not normally a super outdoorsy person, but I can appreciate the beauty of nature as much as the next person. Honestly, it's hard not to with this view. We're standing on an outlook over a deserted beach that seems to stretch for miles in either direction. Long grass blows in the wind that's gusting up from the ocean below. Not too far behind us, on the other side of the path, a group of gnarled pine trees watches as Josh and I stay side by side, breathing in the brackish scent of salt and sea.

Since it's a Monday and school is back in session, we've seen little to no foot traffic. The quiet up here is otherworldly. And even though at times I start getting in my head about all of it—my feelings for Josh, the fact that I'm not sure what he feels for me, the very real possibility that I will eat my body weight in ice cream tonight when he confirms that he loves Hannah—I also feel this sense of peace, like it's all going to be okay, no matter what happens.

I peek at Josh, who is surprisingly in his element today. Not sure why, but I didn't take him for an avid hiker, yet here he is with a hiking backpack and hydration pack, wearing a soft gray tee, a baseball hat, contacts, and sunglasses. He's staring off at the horizon, at the cloudless, perfect sky, and he's more relaxed than I've ever seen him.

Pulling out my phone, I nudge him with my elbow. "No date is complete without selfie proof." I've found myself spouting random quips about what a date should be. It's not what I would do on a normal first date, but it's a nice little reminder to myself not to get carried away. And just in case Josh is really here to try out his date with Hannah, he will actually get some benefit out of today.

"Is that right?" He steps closer to me and puts his head next to mine, smiling into the camera while I snap a shot of us, the horizon at our backs. "So how am I doing so far?"

Dang, he smells good—clean soap and some sort of spicy deodorant that makes me want to hang out right here a little longer. I could totally use the selfie game as an excuse. We need fifty attempts to get one good shot, don't we? Don't we?!

But instead, I'm a good girl and step away, slipping my phone back into my pack before slinging the bag over my shoulders. I lift my hair away from my neck and fan it. Whew. The sun beating down on us is making me warm (let's go with that, anyway) and I'm starting to glisten (remember, a lady does not sweat —ha!).

"So far …" I tap my tipped chin, pretending to think. "It's a nine out of ten."

"Just a nine?" His tone is playful, and I am here for it. I love seeing him this way, all shyness gone. It's hard to believe I used to find him so quiet and plain. "What would take me to a ten?"

We turn from the bluff and start back on the path, which slopes downward a bit.

"You need to remember to carefully balance fulfilling expectations with surprising your date. You've managed to surprise me, but …" I shrug, a grin on my lips.

"Your expectations haven't been fulfilled?" There's something dangerous in his question, and I'm choosing to ignore the shiver racing up my spine at the husky quality of his voice. "How so?"

I wave my hand through the air. "You told me to wear my bathing suit underneath my clothes, so I assume we are swimming. And yet, we've been hiking up here for hours—no beach in sight."

His chuckle makes my heart feel light. "Once again, Leia, sometimes you just need to have a little patience."

Literally one step later, and the landscape dips and opens up on our right, the path winding its way down the bluff and into a secluded cove with a beach. The sparkling water is inviting in its beauty.

I clap my hands together and can't help the squeal that comes from my lips. (Seriously, I am not that girl, but apparently, something about being around Josh makes me a giddy human.) "Race you!"

Then I'm flying down the path, Josh's laughter trailing behind me as I pick up speed. I peek back and he's hot on my tail, so I start sprinting even faster. The breeze I'm creating blows back my hair as my feet crunch over pebbles and twigs. When my shoes hit softer ground, I finally stop, dropping my backpack into the sand.

I turn and grin at Josh, who has caught up to me. "Glad you could make it, slowpoke."

He shucks his pack from his shoulders as well. "I

probably could have been faster if someone had been fair about the whole thing."

"All's fair in—" I stop before I can say the L-word. "Running and fake dating." I cringe once the words leave my mouth, because there's some part of me (fine, a LARGE part of me … ALL of me) that is just begging Josh to lean in and tell me that this is not, in fact, a fake date.

But he doesn't.

Instead, he studies me for a loooong moment—at least, I assume that's what he's doing. I can't see his eyes behind the sunglasses. Then, finally, a slow smile curls around his lips. "Fine, you win."

He kicks off his shoes and peels off his shirt and I want to shout to no one in particular *YES, I DO! I do win!*

Josh removes his sunglasses and hat, running his hands through his hair (a motion that shows off his arms and abs to great advantage). My mouth is dry and I'm just standing there blinking before realizing that this time he can see me ogling him (because, contacts).

So I focus instead on the water, the impending coolness that's about to envelop me—thank goodness, because I think I need a good cold shock right about now. After removing my shirt, shorts, and shoes, I dig my toes into the warm sand and groan at how good my feet feel to be freed from their confines.

When I turn to back to Josh, I find *him* ogling *me*. Okay, ogling isn't the right word, because he's not looking at me in an *ew-get-your-eyes-off-of-me-you-disgusting-perv* kind of way, but … I don't know.

Let's just say he seems to be a fan of my red string bikini.

Let's also say that I absolutely did not wear this in hopes of getting a reaction out of him (read: I totally did).

I saunter up to him, and push his jaw back into place. "Easy there, dude. You wouldn't want to make Hannah jealous." Then I wink, turn, and sprint for the water.

It takes a few seconds, but then I hear him running after me. And just as I'm closing in on the water, I'm lifted off my feet and let loose another squeal as Josh throws me over his shoulder and carries me like I weigh nothing.

When the water splashes up and hits the backs of my legs, I suck in a gasp at the frigid prickles it makes on my skin. Josh's deep chuckle fills my ears as he walks us both in. The water is up to his waist when he drops me down in front of him. But instead of letting go, I cling to his neck and wrap my legs around him. Without a word, he keeps walking until the water is swooping in against my back and his chest.

It's then that I get the courage to pull back and look at him. I love his glasses, but there's something about being able to look into his eyes with no barriers. I cup his cheeks, the desire to kiss him nearly burning a hole through my insides.

But I meant what I said to Evie. I will not impose myself on him. If he's really in love with Hannah, then doing so would feel wrong, like I'm luring him into something he doesn't want.

If anything is going to happen between us, it's his move—which is something totally foreign to me. And yet, it feels right.

At my touch, Josh grips me tighter and I swear he's about ready to go for it—to dive in, as it were. Which means, of course, that a literal wave chooses that moment to take us under.

Because that's my life, folks.

The water washes over our heads, and we lose our hold of one another before coming up, sputtering and coughing. "Are you okay?" he asks.

"Fine." I cough some more as I trudge for the shore and push my now-salty hair out of my face.

He follows suit, helping me from the water. "I should have seen that wave coming. I'm so sorry."

"No worries." Maybe he was as distracted by me as I was by him. A girl can hope, anyway.

We make our way back to our packs, where Josh pulls out a few shammies. We use them to dry off—now that I've had a good soak, the breeze is freezing. "Brrr." I shiver. "It feels like the planet Hoth." (For all of you non-*Star Wars* nerds, that's the icy planet where Luke Skywalker rides that lizard-looking kangaroo creature in the second original movie.)

"Have I mentioned how cool I think you are for your *Star Wars* knowledge, Leia?" As Josh rubs his shammy all over his chest, a slash of water runs down, disappearing into his abs.

Gah. *Focus, woman!* I force a laugh and turn away to stare at the ocean. The sun won't set for another few hours, but it's much lower in the sky now, glinting off the water in that pre-pre-dusk kind of haze it has. "It's not something I tell many people."

"Why not?"

My body mostly dry, I throw my shirt back on over my head in an attempt to get warm. "It's just not part of the image I've carefully cultivated over the years, I guess."

"Part of the mask you wear, huh?"

I recall the conversation we had at the wedding we crashed a little over three weeks ago. *"You don't have to wear a mask with me, Leia."*

And, for the first time maybe … ever, I'm glad. Relieved. I slide down into the sand and stretch out my legs in front of me. "Yeah, maybe. But I don't mean to be fake."

He sits beside me. We're not touching, but I still feel his presence as if we were. "I don't think you're fake at all. In fact, from the first moment I met you, you have always said what you mean. You don't play games. It's actually one of the things I appreciate most about you." The way he says it is so gentle, his voice floating on the breeze, spinning and buzzing in this place of quiet between us.

Whew, things are getting real. Before I can even consider what I'm saying, I go to my default—joking. "What are the other things? My sharp tongue? Or wait. My bossiness? Or is it the way I don't know how to stop even when I should?"

My banter is rewarded with that small smile of his— the one that means so much more than another man's guffaw.

"While those are all very charming parts of your personality, no." He chuckles, then sobers. "There are a lot of things I appreciate and like, but ... yeah. The realness. It means a lot, especially after ..."

"After what?"

It takes him a while, but eventually he continues. "Remember how I told you that I moved here five years ago after a bad breakup?"

I nod.

Sitting cross-legged, he grabs a stick and starts drawing circles in the sand. "I dated Danielle for nearly two years. Thought she was the one for me. We had a lot of conversations about marriage. I was ready, she wasn't, and that was okay. I was willing to wait." Josh crosses through the circles. "She never really told me why she wasn't ready or what was lacking in our relationship. But one day, out of the blue, she texted me and said that things were over. I thought maybe she had found someone else, but when I finally got ahold of her to confront her, to ask her why, she said she'd always wanted to become an actress and that I was holding her back."

"Wow." Sounds like he dodged a bullet, but given the expression on his face, saying that won't make him feel any better. "And you had no idea she wanted that?"

"None. She'd never told me. I don't understand why she felt the need to withhold her real self and desires from me, but it made me swear to myself that I would never go through that again." He presses on the stick and it snaps in half.

I flinch. "I can understand that." Swallowing, I look

away again. "I guess that's why you love Hannah, huh? She's as open as they come."

"So are you." And then his hand is reaching for mine. I let him hold it. "You may have cultivated an image, as you said, but you can't help but be real, Leia. It's just who you are."

I like the way he sees me. But is what he's saying about me even true? I consider my words before speaking, allowing his thumb to gently stroke my hand in a way that I feel all the way to my toes. It's delicious, this full and complete acceptance, and other than Evie, I honestly can't remember a time I've ever been so secure with someone.

Well, that's not true. Before my dad left, he was my safe place, a calming presence in my life, someone I could be my complete self with. Which is why I never understood how he could just … leave me like he did.

Still, as Evie pointed out, Josh is not my dad. And I have to give him a chance to prove it.

"I want to be everything you're saying, but I don't know if I am." I inhale a deep breath. "After my dad left, I built up a wall to protect myself. I became what was modeled for me."

"And what was that?"

"Strong, indestructible." I tell him a bit about my mom—who she is, who she was. "Being with my dad, she was different. Softer. But I'm not sure that soft woman could have survived his leaving, you know? So she became what she had to—callous, unfeeling—and she taught me to do the same."

His fingers intertwine with mine. "I see your

strength, but I'd never call you unfeeling. Even before we were friends, I saw how you were with Evie."

"Evie has a way of getting under your skin." I chuckle, soft. "She helped me to be more comfortable with friendships. But I've still been closed off when it comes to dating. Real romance." I hazard a glance at him. His jaw is tight, and I can't tell what he's thinking. "It's why I have only dated men like Shane, the guy who asked me out at Java Awakening a week and a half ago."

He grunts, and he's wearing a full-blown scowl on his face. It shouldn't make me so happy, but it definitely sends a shot of pleasure through me. If he's jealous, he really might like me after all.

"Anyway." I wave the thought away. Whatever his feelings toward me, I want to share this with him. "I once asked my mom why my dad left, and she said he wasn't able to handle being with a woman who had ambitions beyond our family. According to her, he thought that she should be something she wasn't. And he changed his mind about her."

"He found excuses—petty ones—to stay home from my business functions and not support me despite promising to do so. At first, he was in our marriage one hundred percent. But eventually, he realized that I wasn't what he wanted after all. He wanted a quiet life and I couldn't give that to him. I didn't want to give that to him. It's just not who I am."

I realize with a start that my cheeks are wet. Sheesh—I can't remember the last time I cried about this. Have I ever, really?

Quickly, I swipe at my face, but not before Josh notices. "Leia …"

Turning my head, I face him and jut out my chin. "It's fine. I'm fine."

"Your dad left and it changed the trajectory of your life." Josh lifts his free hand and thumbs away my tears. "It's okay to not be fine, you know."

I stare into his devastatingly handsome face and bite my lip. "My mom always says that tears are weakness."

"No offense to her, but I think it's a good thing that you're crying. It's your body's way of releasing emotions you've maybe been bottling up." He tilts his head. "Just because your mom says it doesn't make it true. You aren't her."

Squeezing closed my eyes, I shake my head. "That's the thing. According to my dad, I *am*."

"What do you mean?"

I put myself back there—the day when my dad showed back up in my life. "He came to see me just after high school graduation. Said he was sorry he hurt me and that he wanted to be part of my life." My voice is trembling and I hate it, because I've been conditioned to despise weakness. But then Josh pulls me into his arms and I lean my head against his shoulder—and I'm glad I didn't hide my lack of strength from him this time. "Before he could say another word, I told him, without a single tear or quiver in my voice, that he hadn't in fact hurt me and that I never wanted to see his face ever again."

Josh kisses the side of my temple. There's so much said in that simple action that he doesn't need words.

"That's when he shook his head and said quietly, 'She's turned you into a mini version of herself.'"

"And what did you say?"

"I asked him whose fault that was before I twirled and slammed the door in his face." As soon as I'd done it, I'd sunk back against the doorframe to keep from going back out there and throwing myself in his arms all pathetic-like. The man didn't deserve forgiveness and I didn't want him thinking he could waltz back into my life and get kudos just for finally showing up. "And now, for the first time in fourteen years, he's tried contacting me again, through my mom. Apparently, he wants to see me."

Josh's breathing is even and steady. "Do you want to see him?"

"No. I don't know." I swallow. "But I don't want to give him another chance to come into my life just to leave it again."

"Leia, any man who would leave you is a fool."

At Josh's whispered words, the dam breaks, and a flood of tears that have been bottled up for more than twenty years comes rushing out.

And Josh, sweet man that he is, holds me upright so I don't drown.

A FEW HOURS LATER, Josh has got a fire going on the beach. The flames lick out and up into the sky, framing the solitude with gentle sparks that light the night.

We've just finished the picnic Josh packed—sandwiches, fruit, and boxed wine—and now we're lying on a blanket in the sand side by side looking up at the stars. We haven't talked about what I shared or the way I soaked his shirt with my tears. Instead, our conversation over dinner was filled with laughter, teasing. Exactly what I needed after the expenditure I deposited in the emotional bank.

His fingers find my hand. "Kayla?"

"Hmm?" My body feels warm, fuzzy, and I know it's not the alcohol. It's Josh. He's got this crazy ability to make me feel ... calm. Like I can rest. In fact, I might have fallen asleep after my confessional, snuggled against his chest. I woke to him stroking my hair. It was the most amazing feeling in the world.

But then, he pulled away and we ate and chatted some more while the sun went down. He asked if I was enjoying myself and I told him he'd planned the perfect date—and that Hannah was going to love it.

What? I had to say it.

I had to know if this is just practice for him, or if what I'm feeling between us is real.

It feels real to me, especially now, with his solid form pressed against mine, his scent enfolding me in the darkness, only the fire and the moon providing any light on the deserted beach where it's just me and him and the stars.

He hasn't said anything back to me, so I try again. "What, Josh?"

Then he shifts so he's on his side, his head propped up with one arm. And with that movement, his eyes are riveted on me, and the calm I felt earlier disappears. My pulse jumps and my body thrums at his nearness—and I know without a shadow of a doubt that I am falling in love with this man.

It hasn't been a *jump-out-of-an-airplane* kind of fall. It's been a gradual one, like a leaf breaking free of its branch and floating to the ground. The wind of my own resistance blew the leaf here and there, but now?

I've got no choice.

I'm opening my arms, surrendering to the free fall. Come what may.

His gaze sweeps over me like liquid—hot, molten liquid. "You've given me feedback on the date, which I appreciate. But you never told me …"

"What?"

"If that kiss was any good."

My body stills.

That kiss. He doesn't have to tell me which one he means. It's only the one that changed everything.

"Oh. Well …" IT WAS AMAZING sticks in my throat. Because even though I suspect his feelings for me go deeper than friendship, I'm still not positive.

"It's okay if it wasn't." He pauses. "But if not, then maybe we should practice more."

Does he know what he's doing to me right now? "I'm not sure that's a good idea."

Because I don't want practice.

I want the real thing.

"How will I learn if you don't teach me?" And there's something so sincere in his gaze, in the way his fingers find my face and his thumb traces my jaw, the trail of his touch like a warm feather on my skin.

I close my eyes, swallow against the dryness in my throat. "Josh, we …" Forcing my eyes back open, I allow our gazes to connect again. "Your kissing was fine."

"Just fine?" His smile teases me.

But I'm not in a teasing mood. "More than fine. I just …" I lick my lips. "You shouldn't practice on me. Not when it's Hannah you want to kiss."

"Kayla."

"What?" I hate the slight anguish in my voice.

"I don't want to kiss Hannah."

My heart stops, right there on that beach. Bam. I'm a dead woman. "What?"

"Hannah is just a friend. It's *you* I'm crazy about."

Can it be true? But … "You hired me to help you date her."

"I never actually said that."

I think back on our conversation and my eyes widen. He's right. I just … assumed. Not that he contradicted me. "So what has all of this been about?"

Please, please, please …

"I've liked you for years, Kayla—basically since that first time you waltzed into Java Awakening and asked me to recommend something on the menu that would, and I quote, blow your freaking mind."

I laugh softly, touched that he would remember it even if I don't.

He continues. "I liked you, but I was never brave enough to do anything about it. When I saw the opportunity to spend extra time with you by being your client, I took it." He swallows hard, clearly uncomfortable. "I'm sorry if you think I lied to you. It's just … you never noticed me before. Never thought of me like that. I know I'm not really your type or whatever, but I don't know. I thought if you could teach me to be more like the guys you normally go for, then maybe I'd have a shot at being with you."

Is he serious? Doesn't he know that he's a thousand times better than those guys? He's real, honest, good, and he's drawn me in with his charming wit, with the steadiness in his gaze that makes him instantly trustworthy, with the very essence of who he is—and who I am when I'm around him.

It's scary and thrilling all at once.

"Josh—"

"Let me finish. Please."

Oh. Okay, then.

"My whole life, I've been looking for a love like my grandparents had. Their house was filled with joy—so different from the house where I grew up. I liked the calm, the peace of it, and I decided then and there that I wanted that. I wanted the same life they had. Their life was all very vanilla, which isn't a bad thing—it worked for them. But it made me think that my life had to look exactly like that in order to be happy." He smiles softly. "Then you burst into Java Awakening and I suddenly realized that life can have color. Flavor. Don't get me wrong—I still want a simple love, simple pleasures, simple nights at home watching movies, just being together. But you've shown me that I don't want to settle for vanilla when I could have pistachio or birthday cake or Rocky Road."

And I can't help myself. I trace the smile lines at the corner of his mouth with my index finger. "Are you saying that I make things difficult?" (Get it? Rocky road? No? Just me?)

He chuckles in that quiet way of his—the one that drives me crazy. "Leia, you make things more interesting. Funnier. Brighter. More beautiful. And you challenge me. You make me want more, want to *be* more, than I did. Before you came along, I was settling and I didn't even know it."

Oh my gosh, kill me now. Is this what I've been missing all of these years while pretending to be satisfied with guys who only want one thing because that's all I was willing to give them—because my heart was locked up in a tower of my own making?

"Say something." His voice is filled with pleading, raw. "Please."

"There's really only one thing to say." My fingers find his bottom lip. "I really think that you should kiss me now."

His eyebrows form a V. "Are you saying that as my coach?"

I take a deep breath. Here goes … everything. "I'm saying it as a woman who has tried very hard not to want you, and is finally waving her white flag." I pause. "I surrender, Josh."

And there's this look of awe that passes over Josh's

features before he lowers himself toward me. In a flash, his lips are on mine and I gasp at the shock of it—because this is not the sweet kiss he gave me in the Java Awakening kitchen.

There's nothing tentative about this one. This kiss is strong, powerful.

Masterful.

With the sway of the ocean as our background music, our lips part and Josh's tongue glides along my own, partaking and imparting in equal measure. My body alternates between fire and ice, and just when I think I can't stand the pleasure curling through me, I press closer and dive in for more. His thumb strokes my cheek and his lips take mine captive again and again … and again.

Then Josh's lips leave mine stranded, but he doesn't abandon me. Instead, his mouth travels to my neck, staying there for a while before moving down to my shoulder. The stubble on his jaw burns a pathway across my collarbone and I'm not sure even Sherman's March to the Sea can rival it.

A moan rumbles from somewhere deep inside of me, and Josh's kisses grow less precise, more frantic as he swoops toward my mouth again. And when he finally pulls back and sits up, breathing hard, I push myself upright and climb onto his lap, tugging his head down so I can ring his ear with kisses. Then I blow a stream of cool air his way—to ignite his senses, to bring them to life.

To tell him I'm not ready to stop. That I'm his, and he's mine, and we are all that matter.

His breathing grows even more ragged as he wraps his arms around me. I've never felt this kind of power before, not even in the courtroom. And yet, it's a shared power, a give and take, because he's doing the same thing to me.

All of the control that I've cherished? It no longer exists, and I am one thousand percent okay with that.

As my lips continue their exploration of him, they move down his neck, to the skin just below the collar of his T-shirt, to the soft hollow between his clavicle and his neck. His skin is warm and salty under my lips as blood whooshes in my ears. I cannot think, cannot feel beyond this moment—beyond Josh, the man I finally, fully admit that I want.

I'm done hiding myself away.

As our mouths connect again, my hands settle on his chest. His heart is pounding as much as mine as I pull back to look into his eyes.

"Kayla." He moves the strap of my shirt just enough to press a kiss into my skin. "Is this real?"

"Mmm." It's all I can say in response.

Then he's kissing my lips again, and we are a haze of light and pounding hearts and an explosion of nerves until—

"Hey, Mom! Over here's a great spot!"

Gasping, I fall away from Josh. We untangle ourselves and he yanks down his shirt before a family with two kids comes strolling around the bend.

As the family sets up a blanket to look at the stars, Josh douses the fire in the pit. I pull my knees into my chest. My heart is still pounding and my mind is whirling with all the implications of what just happened.

Not just physically—though that was incredible—but in my soul.

Because deep down I know I've reached the point of no return.

But when Josh turns, pushes a hand through his hair, and smiles sheepishly at me in the moonlight, I have no wish to go back.

fourteen

. . .

NEW RELATIONSHIPS ARE FUN.

The kissing. The cuddling. The sweet nothings.

Did I mention the kissing?

Because kissing Josh has become my new favorite past-time. With all the training we've done over the last few weeks, I could get a gold medal in the Kissing Olympics.

The irony is that I've never been busier. Between all the jobs coming in—about fifty percent of my first dating coach meetings turn into actual clients—and working shifts at Java Awakening, there shouldn't be time to spend making out with Josh.

But we've gotten creative. (Closing up the coffee shop when we've worked the same shift is a particularly creative venture … even if it takes twice as long as it should.)

It's not like all we do is kiss. We also talk a lot— about everything. I've discovered his favorite color is white (which I argue is actually the absence of color, but I digress), he had a pet turtle growing up (because his mom was allergic to everything else), and he hates to read because he's got dyslexia (but he does like audiobooks).

He's been super supportive of my new business, bringing me meals from this cute Italian place we discovered when I'm working late into the night (although he often proves to be a distraction) and chatting on the phone when I'm driving home from a client meetup. Thankfully, he's not the jealous type who doesn't want me hanging out with guys, so long as I don't use the same flirting-slash-kissing teaching methods I did on him. (I reassured him he's the only one who gets the pleasure of that particular technique.)

All of this adds up to me only getting four or five hours of sleep at night, which is how I find myself nearly dozing off as I wait for the espresso machine at work to brew some java for a forty-something ballerina in a full-blown tutu.

"Kayla."

I startle back awake and knock the mug over. It crashes to the floor and shatters. Cursing under my breath, I turn to find Hannah standing there, her cute little face screwed up into a frown. "Sorry," I mumble as I dart into the kitchen to find a broom in the closet.

I've only got to hold it together for a few more minutes before closing. Then Josh is picking me up and we're heading to Evie's new house—which she moved into last weekend—for a little housewarming get-together. It'll be the first time Josh is meeting Evie's boyfriend and hanging out with my housemates for longer than a few minutes. I wonder if he will be shy or feel right at home.

When I get back to the area behind the counter, Hannah is making the ballerina's drink for me.

"Thanks, girl," I say.

She acknowledges me with an eyebrow lift. Things have been a bit strained with her since Josh and I started dating. Josh says they are just friends, but I think my instincts are right about her liking him as more than that, and I feel kind of guilty for stealing him away—even though he never actually liked her in that way. Still, I've told Josh we shouldn't flaunt our relationship in front of her, just in case.

I clean up the mess I made, sweeping broken mug pieces into the dustpan and tossing them into the trash, then snag the mop and swipe up the spilled brew (and yes, I'm aware that this is not the first time I've had to do this!). By the time I've got it all cleaned up, Hannah is making the rounds, gently reminding the lingering customers that we are closing. I start the rote process of wiping counters and cleaning the espresso machine.

Just then, Josh breezes through the door, looking all too handsome in a pair of jeans and a casual green button-up. Our eyes find each other, and his resulting smile dazzles.

Hannah pulls up short when she sees him. "What are you doing here?"

"Paperwork. I'll be in my office." As he passes me, he waggles his eyebrows—code for "get into my office ASAP so I can kiss you senseless."

Got it, Boss.

I turn to tell Hannah I'll be right back, but before I can, she crosses her arms over her chest and widens her stance. "Kayla, can I talk to you about something?"

"Um, sure." I do everything in my power to not glance at the kitchen door that Josh just breezed through. Goodness, you'd think it had been days since I'd seen him instead of just hours. (Because he maaaaay have come to see me on my lunch break so we could make out in my car—and yes, eat too. But the kissing was a lot more noteworthy.)

"I just …" Hannah frowns. "Josh and I have been friends a long time. He's one of the sweetest guys I've ever met. Super loyal. And I don't want to see him get hurt."

What is she implying? "I don't want that either."

"Then …" She looks at the ceiling, pursing her lips before fixing her attention on me again. "If you were any kind of decent woman, you'd stop messing with his heart, Kayla."

Whoa, what? "What makes you think I'm messing with his heart?"

She flicks her fingers in the air. "I know about this thing you've got going on. And, sorry to say, but it's never going to last. You're just … too different."

Geez, Hannah. And here I thought you were the nice one. Still … maybe she really *is* saying it as a friend, not a jealous wannabe girlfriend. Because from what I can tell, there's no malice in her eyes, just pure unadulterated concern.

Either way, she's wrong. "Haven't you ever heard of opposites attracting?"

"There are opposites, and then there's you guys." She harrumphs. "Maybe you're interested in him right now, but you don't want the same things in life. Even though I don't know you all that well, it's clear that you're the kind of woman who will never be satisfied with a quiet life—and that's all Josh wants."

Her words drive a knife into my heart, making it hard to breathe. "You're right. You *don't* know. Now, if you'll excuse me." I pivot away from her and march through the kitchen door, trying to ignore unbidden visions of it smacking Hannah on the swing back.

It doesn't take long to reach Josh's office, but I hesitate before knocking because there's a buzzing in my back pocket. Good. Fine. Yes. I need a distraction.

And there are two waiting for me on my phone.

The first is good—very good. A text from Jennifer reads: *Finally got my brother to commit to a meeting with you! He'll be in town a week from tonight. Can you do drinks at 7 pm in LA?*

I consider my schedule, can't remember anything. So I type out a response, swift and smooth. *Absolutely! Just text me the address and I'll be there.*

She replies with the address and another message: *I can't wait to hear how it goes! Oh, my brother did ask if you could bring a date, to make things less awkward. *eye roll* I told him you have a bf and are a professional, so it's not like you're going to hit on him, but I think he'd like the assurance anyway. Only if it works out for Josh, though.*

Hmmm. I reply: *Not sure if he can get away from the coffee shop, but we'll see.*

Then, swallowing hard, I flip over to the other text—the one from Mom. *I'm sorry to be the bearer of bad news, but in my most recent call with your father (who I finally threatened with legal action if he doesn't stop contacting me), I may have let it slip that you have a new business. Don't be surprised if he finds your social media profile and DMs you.*

Seriously? There are so many things I want to text in reply.

But at that moment, the door flies open and Josh is standing there looking all sexy, so I shove my phone back in my pocket. He snags me around the waist, pulls me into the office, and shuts the door before pressing me up against the backside of it and giving me a long-awaited (read: three hours and forty-two minutes) kiss.

I'm oh so tempted to clear off a spot on his desk and show him just how much I missed him, but then there's Evie's housewarming party ... and we probably shouldn't be late.

Still, we have a little time, so we linger there at the door for several minutes before he pulls back, leaving me breathless. "Hi," he whispers.

I giggle. "Well, hello there, Solo." (If I'm Princess Leia, then he's totally Han Solo, and I freaking love having dorky nicknames for each other—something I never thought I'd say.)

"I heard you come to the door and thought you'd never come in, so I took matters into my own hands."

"I can see that." I grin, but it wobbles when I think of my mom's text. Of Hannah's words in the lobby.

Suddenly, it all feels like … a lot.

"Whoa. Hey." He brushes a tendril of hair away from my face. "What's wrong?"

I'm not going to tell him what Hannah said—I don't want to make things awkward between them given their friendship and working relationship. But I do fill him in on what my mother wrote.

"I'm sorry." He steps back, gives me space. "How do you feel about that?"

I appreciate this—that Josh hasn't pushed me to call my father despite Dad's persistence. He knows how much my dad's leaving hurt me, and has said if I ever want to do something about it, he'll be here to support me through that.

"Honestly? I don't really want to think about it. I just kind of want to bury my head in the sand and run away from it." I push my index fingers through the front belt loops on his pants and tug him toward me. My arms slide around his neck and the smell of fresh shampoo and coffee beans surround me as his hands find my waist again. "And you make an excellent distraction."

"Always happy to oblige." He smiles, but doesn't swoop in and kiss me again like I long for him to do. "As for running away, I have an idea."

"Do tell."

He tilts his head, studies me. "Next week, there's this *Star Wars* convention in Los Angeles, and I've heard good things. Maybe we could get a hotel and have some alone time in between parading around like lunatics with like-minded nerds."

There's something in his eyes—he's unsure if he's asking too much.

But the thought of being alone with him? Um, yes, please. Because how amazing would it be to cuddle on the couch without his stinky roommates asking if they can horn in and play the X-Box? Or kiss to our heart's content without worrying that one of my housemates will pop her head inside my room (believe me, it's happened!)?

"Joshua Gregory, that sounds … unreal."

"Yeah?"

"I mean, I'm not so sure about the convention part." I make a face. "But for you, I suppose I could come out as a *Star Wars* nerd publicly."

"That might just be the sexiest thing you've ever said."

We both laugh and then our laughter turns to kissing again as I dream about the weekend away. "Oh!" I pull away, my eyes wide.

"What?" He blinks rapidly.

"I can't believe I forgot. I've got a meeting scheduled somewhere in L.A. next Saturday night. So this is perfect." I fill him in on the meetup with Jennifer's brother. "Would you mind coming with me, to ease her brother's mind? I guess he's super shy around women and having another guy there would go really far in getting him to sign on with me."

"Yeah, I could do that." His brow furrows. "This is the guy who could be the key to getting you in with a bunch of celebrity and producer types, right?"

"Exactly. And if I land this client and it leads to

others, then I might start making enough to hire some help. Expand the business."

"Then sign me up, Leia."

Ha! Take that, Hannah. There's nothing "quiet" about going to drinks at an upscale bar in L.A., but Josh just agreed to do it without hesitation.

"You're the best, Solo." I press one last kiss to his mouth. "I guess we'd better get going to Evie's."

Our evening at my bestie's is perfect, albeit a little sad. But she's done up the place so well, and she and Connor look so happy together, kissing in the kitchen when she thinks no one is looking (which is ridiculous, because between me, Josh, my four housemates, and Shelby's best friend Eric crammed into her tiny "great room," without a doubt someone will see them).

Connor cooks us his mom's lasagna and tells us all about his romance novel, which releases in nine months. He's already started writing the sequel. Evie hangs on his arm, adoring and so in love that the old Kayla would have thought it rather disgusting. (Not really … I just would have been hiding my own pangs of longing behind the disgust.)

But as I look around the table in Evie's backyard, which is lit with these adorable little twinkle lights Connor hung for her, my heart feels full—as does my hand, because Josh hasn't let go of it almost all night. More than one of my housemates has commented on how "cute" we are, and I find that I don't mind the teasing one bit.

We *are* cute, no matter what Hannah says.

If we were really so wrong for each other, would it

feel like this—so effortless? Josh has had no trouble shooting the breeze with each of my friends, even Alexis, who can be difficult when she wants to be. I whisper in his ear to ask her about her favorite movies, and then she's off to the races and no one can get her to shut up (might have something to do with the beer she keeps slamming too, but that only makes her more outrageous than usual).

At one point, Evie pulls me aside. "I love seeing you so happy. You guys are good for each other."

That means a lot coming from her. You can't get more opposite than Connor and Evie—him the former smooth-talking bad boy, her the conservative and quirky editor who grew up on a dairy farm in Iowa—and they're somehow making it work. More than, in fact. If my instincts are right, they'll be engaged by Thanksgiving if not before.

So what does dumb ole Hannah know?

Nothing.

Then why can't I get her words out of my brain? *"It's never going to last. You're just … too different."*

Maybe because I know that my parents were good for each other too—until they weren't.

But Josh and I are not my parents.

And, as I look across the room to see Josh teaching Lauren, Shelby, and Eric a few swing dancing moves, *that's* the mantra I choose to repeat in my mind instead.

I'm still repeating it when Josh brings me home, gives me a sweet kiss good night, and tells me he will handle all the arrangements for our weekend away.

fifteen

· · ·

WHO KNEW cosplay could be so exhausting?

Or maybe that's just the fact I've barely slept all week, rearranging my schedule so I could make this trip to L.A. happen. But being at the *Star Wars* Forever convention all day (after a super early drive to town) has me dead on my feet as Josh and I wheel our suitcases to our hotel room on Friday.

I've gotta admit—I was a bit skeptical about the whole convention thing, but it was really quite fun. The best part was surprising Josh with the costumes I bought. I've had to keep myself under control at the sight of him in his Han Solo trousers, boots, vest, and— my favorite part—low-slung gun belt. (What? It's hot.)

And he seemed to enjoy my version of Princess Leia's slave outfit (read: he couldn't keep his hands off me either).

Josh arrives at the room and unlocks it, then pushes open the door. It's not the fanciest hotel, but it is nice, with a lovely view of downtown. Since we'll be here all weekend, Josh opted for a two-bedroom suite with a small living room and kitchenette. (And when I teased him about not wanting to sleep in the same room as me, he got very serious, said he didn't want me to feel any pressure to take things to the next level. I about melted right then and there.)

The sight of the comfy couch has my tired muscles relaxing. I try to cover my unbidden yawn, but can't.

He looks at me. "Do you need to head for bed?"

Shaking my head, I force my eyes to stay open. "It's only eight o'clock."

"But you're tired, Leia." His lips hitch up. "You had a busy week, a busy day. You should rest."

He's the sweetest man alive. But I'm determined. "We actually have time alone tonight and I refuse to waste it. Just give me time to shower. That will wake me up."

"All right." Before I can move, he takes my suitcase to the first bedroom and pops it inside.

I follow.

"I'll go shower too and we can meet out here in fifteen minutes," he says.

"Sounds like a plan." I sink back against the door frame. "Though I will be sad to see the Han costume go."

The sound of Josh's chuckle shoots me through with a bit of heat, a bit of energy. "We're wearing our costumes tomorrow too, aren't we?" He places one arm above me and leans in, tracing my bare stomach with his fingertip.

I shiver. Okay, definitely more awake now. "Of course."

"That's good. I kind of liked seeing all of those guys with their eyes bugging out at the sight of us together, wondering how a guy like me landed a girl who is ten thousand times out of his league."

"Whatever." I roll my eyes.

"I'm serious. Just look at you. You are the most beautiful woman I've ever seen." Reverence transcends his features. "Then look at me. You're so much more sophisticated—and did I mention gorgeous?"

His words have me legit blushing (and I don't blush!). "So? You're hot."

As his eyebrows lift in disbelief, I shake my head. "Do you know what the hottest thing about you is? Your humility. You have no freaking idea how attractive you are, and that lack of an ego is refreshing." I waggle my brows. "And then there are these abs …" I trail my fingers down his shirt.

His cheeks turn red. "You like those, do you?"

"They're my new best friend." I laugh, then grow serious. "But Josh, what you're saying about leagues, I don't see it. I see you and me, and we're just Josh and Kayla. You can't always put people in boxes."

"I know. You're right." He massages the back of his neck. "I'd better let you shower. See you soon." Then he kisses me quick and turns to snag his own stuff.

My head spinning from the activities of the day, I shut my door, remove my costume, and hop in the shower. When I'm out, I clear some steam off the mirror, staring at myself. My skin is flushed and shiny, my hair wet around my shoulders.

I dig in my suitcase and pull out a few clothing options. There are my cute leggings and soft tunic shirt I bought to lounge in this weekend.

Or there are the sweats and comfy T-shirt that I actually wear to bed on a regular basis.

Josh has never seen me without makeup. This raw, this vulnerable.

But even though I hesitate for a moment to show him the "real me," I pop the sweats on and head for the living room, where Josh is sitting on the couch. He's wearing the exact outfit he did to speed dating and his glasses are back. His hair is damp and I can smell him from here. (And it is good, my friends. It is good.) The TV screen is on but muted, and he's scrolling on his phone.

I plop down next to him. "Whatcha doing, handsome?"

He startles a bit, but when he sees me, his eyes light up. "You look more awake."

"I look like a drowned rat," I joke.

But he just buries his nose in my damp hair and inhales. "You smell amazing."

"Likewise."

When he pulls back, he clears his throat. "And as for what I was doing … I wanted to show you something." He's suddenly serious and a bit fidgety. Why is he nervous?

Something twists in my stomach. "Okay."

He angles his phone toward me so I can see the

screen. "I've been looking at houses."

"You finally saved up the down payment?"

"Yeah."

"Josh, that's huge. Congratulations!" I pull his hand —and the phone—closer. On the screen is an adorable craftsman-style house with three bedrooms and two baths on the outskirts of town. The architecture is modest and simple, with a wide-open porch flanked by thick tapered columns. Large bay windows frame the front of the house. I'll bet they let in a lot of light.

The house is basically a representation of Josh.

"I love it." I let go of his hand and glance at him. "Are you going to make an offer?"

"I want to go look at it in person." He puts the phone face down on the couch beside him and messes with his glasses for a moment—a sign he *is* actually nervous. But why?

Surely he doesn't need my affirmation? I'll give it anyway. After all, this is his big dream—and I'm stoked for him that he's achieving it sooner than he thought. "That sounds wise."

"Kayla …" He shifts so he's facing me, his arm draped along the back edge of the couch, his hand playing with a tendril of my wet hair as he looks at me. "Would you go with me? I know you're busy, but I can work around your schedule."

"Sure. Of course." I love that he values my opinion. But as he keeps watching me without saying a word, my mouth forms an O. "Wait. Why do you want me to go with you?"

Josh glances away for a minute, his lips pursing into

a brief frown. Then he pivots his gaze back to me, a determination in his eyes that wasn't there before. "I don't want to buy it if you don't like it."

"Because …?"

He huffs. "You're going to make me say it, aren't you?"

"Say what?" But deep down, I know. And I'm not sure how I feel about it.

"That I don't want to go to the trouble of buying a place where you can't ever see yourself living."

And there it is. My chest tightens for a moment, but then … peace. What is this otherworldly calm? "Are you asking me to move in with you?"

"Not yet."

Yet.

Yet.

"I know we haven't been together long, and maybe this is premature. It probably is." He groans and shakes his head. "I don't want to screw this up or scare you away. But I'd kind of like to know where you stand on … marriage."

Whoa. I swallow. "I … well, I don't think I ever thought I'd get married. I didn't exactly have the best example."

"I can understand that." He's saying the words, but his eyes look … disappointed. Sad.

Should I tell him the rest? *Yes.* Something deep whispers in my soul, tells me I may always regret it if I don't speak my truth. The whole truth. And nothing but the truth. "The idea of committing myself fully to someone who might love me one minute and then wake up one day and realize that I'm not what he wants after all—like my dad did to my mom—is completely terrifying."

"Trust me, I get that. I have the same fears." Right. Because Danielle basically did the same thing to him. "But do you think there's a way forward, past the fear?"

"I ... I don't know." I tilt my head. "If you've got any ideas, I'm all ears."

Josh licks his lips and I swear I hear every single noise in the room at that moment. The static buzz of the TV. The distant murmurings of the neighbors on one side of our walls. The dripping of the kitchenette faucet.

And the pounding of both of our hearts.

He slides forward, looping my legs over his and caressing my cheek with his thumb. "How do we move forward? We say what we mean. We stay real. And we promise to be there and support each other through everything. Big stuff. Small stuff. The in-between stuff. We stay and we fight and we do whatever it takes to make this work."

Oh, this man. He knows exactly what I need to hear —and he isn't just saying it. I can sense his sincerity with every fiber of my being. And I have no choice but to be sincere back. "You remember what you said to me on the beach? About me being real?"

"Yeah."

Swallowing hard against a sudden dryness in my throat, I continue. "I'm the realest version of myself when you're around. And that ... well, it scares me, because it means I'm vulnerable. Open. Dangling on a precipice and falling. But I'm starting to think that maybe it's better to balance on the edge of the unknown, if it means that we get this. If it means I get you." I take a deep breath. "And if that someday leads to marriage, well … I'm open to it."

He leans in until our noses touch. "Leia—Kayla." Then Josh kisses me slow and sweet, and there's a promise in it. His kiss ignites me, turns me upside down, inside out, and makes me realize that nothing before this moment matters. All that matters is me and Josh and this love building and pulsing between us.

For the first time, I think forever might be within my arms.

And I never want to let go.

sixteen

. . .

IF POSSIBLE, Day 2 of the *Star Wars* Forever convention is even nerdier—and more fun.

There's something about being crammed into a convention center auditorium with thousands of fellow fans, many of them dressed as characters, watching clips from our favorite movies and waiting with bated breath to hear from some of the newest movies' stars.

We're standing and clapping along with some music. Here, I'm hiding behind my Leia costume, my Leia makeup—and yet as Josh loops his arm around my waist and pulls me in for a selfie, I've never felt more myself.

More … free.

A few months ago, I would have murdered him in his sleep if he'd posted a selfie like that on social media, but just yesterday I officially outed myself on my dating coach profile. It was a picture of Josh and me in cosplay, kissing in front of the convention center, and I captioned it:

Rule 23 of dating success: Find someone who helps you to be your true self.

Despite the audience surrounding us, I turn and give him another kiss. When he pulls back, I see love in his eyes—love that's even deeper after last night. Or maybe it was there all along, and I just didn't see it.

And even though we haven't said the words yet, they don't scare me like they did.

The speakers come on stage to swelling applause, and for the next hour, we listen to the cast talk about their adventures while filming, as well as what might be up next in the *Star Wars* franchise. When the speech is done, we filter out of the auditorium and into the exhibition hall, where we spend hours admiring the various memorabilia and I win a Yoda stuffy with my amazing basketball skills. (I promptly found a child and gave it to her because she was the most adorable little Princess Leia in the whole place.)

For a late-lunch-early-dinner, Josh buys us both a Ronto Wrap and a strange blue drink, which we enjoy together near a window that showcases the cloudless October sky.

I polish off my wrap and check my phone. "We'd better get back to the hotel to shower and get ready for my client meeting tonight."

"You sure you don't want to wear your Leia outfit?" Josh's teasing smirk makes an appearance.

"I'm not sure how the really shy guy who is reticent

to even meet with me in the first place would feel about me showing in this getup."

"He'd probably swallow his tongue." My boyfriend (love that word!) winks at me. "Then again, he will probably do that no matter what you wear."

I stand and clear the table. "I hope he's not too shy. It sounds like he'll be in town for the next few months, and I can't bring you to all of my meetings with him."

Josh joins me and takes the tray, which he tosses in a nearby garbage can. Then he pulls me close. "I'd happily go if it means your business succeeds."

"You are the best guy in the world." I fist his shirt and raise an eyebrow. "And I think we should finish this conversation back in our room."

His eyes widen. "Yes, ma'am." He snatches my hand and drags me toward the entrance, both of us laughing. I'd say we were probably attracting lots of attention—because Han and Leia don't normally giggle like fools—but there's a Storm Trooper being handcuffed by a police officer in one corner and a drunk Wookiee singing show tunes in another.

So, yeah.

We're almost to the exit, when a man steps in front of us, hands held out. "Kayla."

I go absolutely still—because I know that voice. That voice used to tell me stories at bedtime. Used to calm my fears when I had a nightmare. Used to explain to me the difference between a Jawa and an Ewok.

That voice has been absent from my life for so long—and yet, I recognize it.

But I barely recognize the man who it belongs to. My

gaze stumbles over him. His hair is nearly gone and what's left is peppered with gray. His middle is rounder and he now wears glasses. Unlike everyone else here, he's dressed in street clothes.

And there's a desperation in his eyes that's utterly haunting.

I can feel Josh's gaze on me, questioning. Clearing my throat, I finally speak. "What are you doing here, Dad?"

Josh presses a supportive hand to the small of my back. He's got me.

"I've tried contacting you through your mother." My father frowns. "Did she … did she give you my messages?"

The music from the convention hall now seems a thousand times louder than it did, and the pounding reverberates in my skull. I want to ask Dad if we can take this outside, but he might see that as an invitation, a promise that I'm going to consider talking with him.

And I can't. I won't.

Letting Josh in is one thing.

Letting a man who has already hurt me—who has already proven that he won't stick around—is quite another. And I'm not stupid.

I tilt my chin up in defiance. "She did." I let the words sit. Let him know that I knew about his requests —and ignored them.

He sighs and scrubs a hand down his face. I notice the wrinkles invading his skin, which droops at the corners of his eyes. He looks a lot older than his fifty-five years.

I cross my arms over my chest and swing my long Leia ponytail back over my shoulder. "Like I said … why are you here, Dad?"

"I saw your social media post and figured out you were attending the convention. I've been looking for you all day."

I should have guessed. Mom warned me that he knew about my new business and was probably following me on social media. "Why now? Are you sick or something?" Isn't that why a lot of people contact loved ones they've kicked to the curb? They want some sort of reconciliation, peace for their troubled souls, before they die.

There's a tiny twinge of dismay at the thought, but I push it away. He doesn't deserve my pity.

He shakes his head. "No. I …" Glancing at our surroundings, he takes a step closer—a move that has me tensing up. "Can we go somewhere and talk?"

My insides are all twisted. "No, we can't. I don't want to talk to you." Now. Or ever. "Besides, I have a meeting in Beverly Hills in an hour and a half, and have to get ready for that. Plus, traffic."

"Okay. What about tomorrow? Will you still be in town? I live here now and—"

"I *will* still be in town, but I'm spending time with Josh."

As if noticing my boyfriend for the first time, my dad glances at him, extends a hand. "I'm Rick Clark. You must be—"

"No, Dad." I slap his hand away. "You don't get to waltz in here and pretend like you have a place in my life anymore. You're the one who left, but you don't get to be the one who decides when you return."

He pulls back. "You're right. But if you'd just let me explain …"

"I don't want to hear it. Mom was right about you. You're just a sad, selfish man who never knew what he wanted." The words taste like ash, but I speak them anyway. What other choice do I have?

I know I cried with Josh a few weeks ago on the beach, but I absolutely refuse to give my dad the satisfaction of knowing he reduced me to tears.

"And before you say like mother, like daughter, I just want you to know—I'm proud of that fact. Because being like her helped me to survive you. And I'll keep on surviving you long after today." I breeze past him and head for the exit.

I'm almost there before I realize that I left Josh behind. Turning, I see him talking with my father. His eyebrows are furrowed as my dad hands him something. Then he's hauling himself across the exhibition floor toward me.

"What did he want?"

Josh holds up a card. "He gave me his number in case you changed your mind."

I take the card from him, rip it in half, and toss it into a garbage can. "I won't."

We head back to our hotel, a short walk, in silence, which is fine by me. I'm fuming and have no desire to talk. I need to focus on work, on landing this client. This is how I process—to ignore for a while, to let things simmer and sit.

But I can feel Josh's rising anxiety next to me. A quick glance at him shows his clenched jaw, his set shoulders, the fists at his side.

When we finally get inside our suite, he stops me before I turn toward my room. "Kayla, don't you think …"

I narrow my eyes. "What?"

"I don't know. Just … why don't you have coffee with him and hear him out at least?"

Seriously? "Because the man left me. He doesn't get to come back when it's convenient for him."

Josh massages the back of his neck. "No, I know. But isn't the conflict killing you? Especially when it's within your power to address it."

I get it. He's a peacemaker. "We aren't the same, Josh."

It's never going to last. You're just … too different.

Stupid Hannah. This is not the time for her words to be invading my brain—even if she's right about us being different. But all couples have areas where they aren't the same. Apparently one of mine and Josh's is conflict management. "I just need time."

"But you've had time. Months of him trying to contact you. Do you think maybe you should hear him out?" He studies me. "Maybe it will make you feel better to talk to him."

He just doesn't get it. "I said I need time. So give me time. And space."

Before he can sidle up to me or try to give me a hug or whatever it is he's thinking about doing, I slip away and into my room, shutting the door firmly. Then I strip off my costume, leaving it balled on the floor, and put the shower on the hottest setting it can go. Let it burn my skin. I don't care. I'm made of iron today, and it won't touch me.

I have to focus on my meeting tonight. That's all that matters.

When I step into the water, I hiss between my teeth, but I don't turn it colder.

And I fight the tears welling behind my eyes. The ones that Josh says aren't a weakness. Maybe he's right.

But I'm afraid if I let them come, there will be no stopping them. So I push on my closed eyes with the palms of my hands as water scalds my back.

By the time I'm done, my skin is as red as a tomato, but I am fortified. Ready to forget what happened earlier and reel in a huge client that could change my business forever. I may have been somewhat distracted the last few weeks because of my new relationship, but this meeting—this business—means everything to me.

It means that no one but me controls my destiny.

Seeing my dad reminds me that securing my future is the most important thing I can do.

After doing my makeup and hair, I put on a lacy bra and underwear that make me feel secretly powerful, then pull a red sheath dress from the closet that makes me feel outwardly so. When I'm all tucked in and assembled, I add the finishing touch—my four-inch Jimmys.

The mask is on, secure.

Or maybe this is just me after all.

I am Kayla, hear me roar—and all that.

I step from the room and pull up short. Josh is sitting on the couch, still dressed as Han Solo. His head is in his hands until he looks up at me, worry in his eyes.

My feet carry me forward. "Why aren't you dressed? We need to leave."

"I know. I can get dressed quick." He pats the seat next to me. "Can we talk for a few minutes first?"

Seriously? "No, Josh. I don't have time for that. And there isn't anything to talk about."

His gaze pins me there until I huff. "Fine." My shoes clickety-clack on the tile floor until I reach the rug near the couch and then sit next to Josh. "What's wrong?"

"Kayla, this avoidance … it isn't healthy."

My mouth falls open. How dare he! "You have no idea what I'm going through. Don't pretend you know what's best for me."

"I'm not." He scrubs a hand across his face, up into his hair as he groans. "I'm botching this, I know. I just care about you so much and I hate fighting."

"We wouldn't be fighting if you just left it alone." I cross my arms. "Let me deal with my dad the way I see fit."

"Look, I'm not saying you have to let him back in your life. Just … talk to him. Maybe even forgive him. This unforgiveness is only hurting you."

That's it. I hop up from the couch. "You have no right to say that to me. We've been dating a few weeks and suddenly you think you're an expert on my life?"

And there's hurt there, in his eyes. I hate that I'm the one who put it there, but does he hear himself?

"No, but I'd like to think that I know *you*. Or were

you lying when you said you're the realest version of yourself when you're with me?"

"That's really low of you, to use my words against me."

"It's not a me-against-you thing, Kayla." Removing his glasses, he rubs the bridge of his nose. "It could be us against the world, but you won't let me in. Times like this, when there's conflict, your walls keep going up, and I don't know how to scale them or when they'll come back down. If they ever will. It's just like Danielle all over again."

Did he seriously just compare me to his ex? "That's not fair." I check the clock on the wall. "We don't have time for this. Are you coming to drinks or not? Because we need to go."

"I know your job is important, but so is this conversation. And I don't feel like we've finished it yet, Kayla."

"We can finish it later."

"But will we?"

I throw my hands in the air. "What do you freaking want from me, Josh? I can't do this right now. I have a meeting to get to."

He just sits there, staring at me. "I'll go get ready."

"You know what?" I snatch my purse from the table near the doorway. "Just forget it. I'll go by myself."

"Fine." His lips narrow. "I'm not very good at faking it anyway."

I feel the dig deep in my soul—because apparently, I am. "Enjoy your night snuggled up on the couch alone then."

With one more glance at him, I see that his face is

red, his lips turned down. He's clearly miserable.

I make him miserable.

Just like my mom made my dad miserable—so miserable that he left.

What was I thinking? Josh is just like my dad. I'm just like my mom. We can't avoid it, and I was stupid to think we could.

Maybe who I am with Josh is actually the pretense— the woman I've always wanted to be, but can't. Sooner or later, though, the mask will slip.

And he will leave.

Though I fooled myself into pretending it's not, it is inevitable.

I once asked my mom if there's anything she'd have done differently with my dad. You know what she said? *"I'd have left him first."*

And right now, in this moment, that makes sense. I get it. The idea of waiting around for him to leave me makes my skin crawl. Makes my stomach bottom out.

Makes me want to cry.

And that's how I know that I can't do it anymore.

Josh's voice from last night nags at me. *"How do we move forward? We stay and we fight and we do whatever it takes to make this work."*

But he's not doing that, is he? If so, he'd keep his promise. He'd put on his big boy pants and come to the meeting I actually NEED him at even if he has to fake it till he makes it.

But I won't beg.

At least it only took three weeks and not three years —or ten—for me to realize that this just isn't going to work. That I will always remind him of Danielle, and he will always remind me of my dad. That there is no moving forward from the fear.

But it's fine. I'm fine. We're all fine here.

There's a hole in my heart, sure, but it's only a rip. It'll heal. Better to end this now than when the hole is a gaping wound I can't possibly fix.

I turn on my heel, march back to my room, gather up my stuff, and toss it into my suitcase. My clothes and toiletries are an unwieldy mess. But I'm able to zip the suitcase up, and you can't even tell there's chaos inside.

I wheel the suitcase out into the hallway, to the living room.

Josh's eyes grow wide. "What are you doing?"

"I asked for space, and you just couldn't give it to me. So I'm taking matters into my own hands. This"—I move a finger between us—"is over. And so is my gig at the coffee shop."

"Please don't leave." Josh scrambles up from the couch. "Talk to me, Leia."

"Don't." If he uses that pet name for me and puts his arms around me, I don't think I can do what I know I need to—for both of our sakes. The stupid tears are back, being as pushy as a lawyer with a bone to pick. I beg them to stay put for the time being. "I should have listened to my instincts."

And before I give in to the ache in my chest, I pivot and leave the hotel room, slamming the door behind me.

Shutting it forever on the future I was an idiot to envision.

seventeen

. . .

I DIDN'T GET the job.

Jennifer's brother took one look at me—alone—and turned red, then found a lame excuse to leave before our drinks even arrived at the table. (I mean, did he really have to feed his cat RIGHT THEN?)

Ever since that night almost three weeks ago, I've struggled.

First, word has gotten around that the dating coach can't even keep her own relationship going. (Thanks, random Instagrammer who decided to invade my privacy for whatever reason and show up to interview Hannah at Java Awakening. Josh's "friend" was all too happy to reveal that I'd quit and wasn't around anymore.)

And second, I just can't focus. (I refuse to acknowledge that this is a symptom of a broken heart, but Evie swears that's what is going on.)

Some of my client meetings have gone fine, but

others? Wow, have they flopped badly. The worst was when one of my clumsy clients tripped and grabbed my butt. I may have overreacted and called him a few choice names. Playing back over the scene in my mind, I really do think he touched me by accident. All of my other interactions with him were pleasant, and he was always respectful.

Then there was the whole crying thing … Yes, apparently I make grown men cry.

It's like I can't trust anyone anymore.

Least of all myself.

Well, that's not true. I can trust my friends. Which is why when Evie told me in her *I'm-gonna-pretend-to-be-tough* voice that she, Lauren, and I were going out tonight, I didn't bother arguing.

So here we are, strolling through Balboa Park on a gorgeous Friday evening in late October, eating ice cream even though we're freezing our rears off. But Evie insisted, so that's that.

I spoon a bite of vanilla into my mouth as we walk past gorgeous tall white buildings in the park. The path is lined with mature trees, everything from palms to pines. Other pedestrians wander and mingle, some in a hurry, others lingering like us. "So, what are we celebrating?"

Evie stiffens beside me. She darts a glance at Lauren, whose eyes bulge as she stares at her strawberry cone.

I stop walking. "I was just teasing, since I know you don't need an excuse to get ice cream, Evs." Narrowing my eyes, I study her, walking all innocent-like in her jeans and cute pink blouse. "But now I'm suspicious."

My bestie bites her lip. "Nope, nothing. Just … uh … the fact that you're out of the house finally!"

I snag her elbow before she can squirm away. "Spill it, sister. Did you get another promotion? Sign a big author?"

Her eyes look pained. Oh no. What if she decided to leave, to move back to Iowa after all? It was something she considered earlier this year, but then she got the promotion.

Evie stuffs a bite of cookie dough ice cream into her mouth. "Conn-ah puh-posed." She glances away as if trying to hide from me.

"What?!"

At my squeal, she jumps and drops her ice cream down the front of her shirt. "Aw, man."

Lauren glances between us. "I'm going to go get you some napkins." Then she jogs off.

Evie swipes her fingers at the trickles of melting cream. "I'm seriously like a toddler sometimes."

But I'm not letting her off the hook so easily. "Evie, did you say that Connor proposed?"

Her lips twist into a grimace and her fingers wipe more quickly.

I place my hands on hers to stop their movement. "When?"

She glances up at me, pure chagrin in her features. "Three days ago."

My appetite gone, I toss my unfinished dessert into a garbage can. "Why didn't you tell me sooner?"

Lauren jogs back up with a pile of napkins, as if Evie spilled a whole river of ice cream. "Got some!" She waves them in the air, triumphant. But then she seems to read the mood between us and starts backing away like she's Michael Jackson doing the moonwalk.

I snap my head toward her. "And you knew about this?"

She's quiet—but she doesn't stop moonwalking away.

Rolling my eyes, I march toward her, grab her elbow, and haul her back to Evie, who is now furiously cleaning up her shirt. "Did everyone know but me?"

"Define … everyone," Evie squeaks.

I toss my hands in the air. "Unbelievable." And then, because I just can't deal with this right now, I turn and stride down the path toward a large fountain. It's ringed with red bricks, and there's a main spout of water in the middle that's bright orange in the waning daylight. Several smaller streams of water—colored red—arc inward, as if they're bowing to the orange.

It all tumbles together, building, concentrating, condensing, rippling.

At the sight, the geyser inside of me finally erupts.

My best friend is getting married and didn't tell me. And I know why—she didn't think I could handle it. Maybe she's right. I haven't exactly been open the last three weeks. I told her Josh and I broke up, but didn't tell her why. And then I threw myself into my work, or attempted to anyway.

But now that's failing too.

I've lost control and I desperately want it back. But just like this fountain, I'm a product of the pain, and I don't know how to become myself again.

There's a hand on my back, and when I turn to Evie, she startles. "Kay, are you crying?"

I swipe at my cheeks and shake my head no—then stop. What do I have to hide from Evie? Nothing. She knows everything about me and loves me anyway. So I nod and let the tears come for the second time in the last few months.

"Aw, friend." She grabs me into a fierce hug, and I know when Lauren joins us, because I become a Kayla sandwich. They soothe and they pat and they whisper that it's all going to be okay.

"I'm sorry. I'm sorry." I just keep repeating it, and I don't really know who I'm talking to.

Evie? Myself?

Josh?

No, not him. He wasn't there for me when I needed him. And I haven't heard a word of apology since— haven't heard a word at all—which means he realizes he dodged a bullet with me.

Finally, the tears slow down and I pull away. Lauren hands me a wad of napkins and I wipe my mascara-stained eyes and cheeks. I probably look like a raccoon, but at this point, I don't even care.

Evie walks me to a bench and the three of us sit, me in the middle. "I'm sorry I didn't tell you, Kayla. I wouldn't have told the others before you, except—"

"We forced it out of her," Lauren interrupts. "She came over yesterday to talk to you, but you were at a client meeting. Alexis could tell something was different about her and we bugged her until we figured it out."

I picture the scene and laugh. "I have no doubt it took about two seconds before she caved."

"I'm not good under that kind of pressure." Evie covers her face with her hands before placing them on my knee again. "But I do admit that I was hesitant to tell you. You've been so sad. It feels wrong for me to be so happy."

I sigh and sit back against the bench, the concrete cold against my upper arms. "I would never begrudge you your happiness, Evs."

"I know." Evie pauses, takes a breath, and glances at Lauren before looking back at me. A breeze ripples my hair as I wait for her inevitable question. "Kay, what happened with Josh?"

So I tell them the whole story. When I mention my dad's reappearance, Evie audibly gasps and holds my hand a little tighter. Lauren fidgets beside me, and I don't know if it's because she is the kind of person who can't sit still or if she's thinking of her own life—the fact she doesn't speak with her parents.

I get to the end of the tale. "So I left, because the ending was inevitable."

My friends are silent, and the space between us fills with the sounds of the fountain splashing, kids laughing as they get close to the water and dodge each other, a dog barking at the chaos.

And even though I expected Evie to pipe up, it's actually Lauren who speaks first. "You talk a lot about destiny and control." Her breath shudders in, out, as if she has a personal stake in what she's saying. Maybe she does. "But in my experience, people make their own choices. There is no inevitable. There is only you and Josh and the decisions you make. And it's those decisions—not some mysterious destiny—that can change the course of your life."

"True, but I can't control the decisions *he* makes." I know my argument is weak, but it's all that I have. "I don't want to become my parents."

Evie squeezes my knee again. "Kay, the irony is that you don't want to be controlled by someone else's choice, but you're allowing fear to control your actions instead."

The bottom drops out of my stomach.

She's right.

Totally right.

All these years, I've prided myself on being in control, on running my own life, on being the one to captain my own ship.

But fear has been the ghost captain all along, his icy hands on the wheel, turning and steering it wherever he wanted to go.

"I think I'm going to be sick."

Lauren tosses her arm around my shoulders and holds a napkin under my mouth. "Barf it up, sister."

That makes me laugh—loud. Soon all three of us are in hysterics. A mom with two little kids walks by, eyeing us and ushering her children quickly past as if we've got the bubonic plague and she's afraid of catching it.

But laughter really is the best medicine, especially when it's done in the company of friends.

I incline my head against Lauren's, and Evie leans on

my shoulder. My lips tremble as I puff out one more laugh. "I don't know what to do next."

"Can I add in my two cents?" Evie asks.

"Of course."

"Let love control your actions instead of fear."

"Easier said than done." I pause, frown. "I haven't heard from Josh at all since that night. Not that I blame him, since I basically left the same way his ex did." Without much explanation, because it hurt too much to hash it out.

Because—I can see now—I was afraid he'd talk me out of it.

I was self-sabotaging and I didn't even know it.

"Didn't you tell him you wanted space?" Lauren asks.

"I guess."

"Seems to me he's giving you exactly what you wanted. It's probably killing him to stay away from you."

"You're right."

Lauren shrugs. "Besides, you don't strike me as the kind of woman to wait around for a guy to come knocking with a grand gesture."

"That's all very true." Evie clears her throat, sits up, and tugs at the bottom of her blouse. "But when I said that love should control your actions instead of fear, I wasn't talking about your relationship with Josh."

My eyes dart to hers. And I know exactly what she *is* talking about.

Or rather, who.

"I can't, Evs."

"You can't move forward without making peace with the past. Believe me. I know."

She does. I know she does.

And she's right. I know she is.

But that doesn't mean I have to like it.

eighteen

. . .

ON THE OUTSIDE, I'm Elsa the Ice Queen.

On the inside, though?

I'm melting faster than Olaf the snowman on a summer's day.

Waiting to meet up with your father after years and years apart will do that to a girl.

When I texted him yesterday to set up a meeting time, he responded within minutes. And since it's the weekend, he was able to come down here so I didn't have to rearrange my morning meetings with the few clients I have left.

Now, I'm sitting in the back corner of an old-fashioned diner. Waiting.

I drum my fingers along the shellacked teal tabletop, allowing my mind to zero in on the words Josh said the last time we spoke. *"Look, I'm not saying you have to let him back in your life. Just ... talk to him. Maybe even forgive him. This unforgiveness is only hurting you."*

I hate that Josh was right. But look how far this fear has taken me—I abandoned the man I love.

Yes, love.

It came to me Friday night, when I was listening to Evie explain how Connor proposed to her. He'd written her a letter that mirrored Mr. Darcy's proposal from *Pride & Prejudice*, saying things about how his feelings will not be repressed any longer, how he ardently admires and loves her, et cetera. (Sorry, folks, I have barely even seen the movie, much less read the book. This is all the detail you're going to get from me.) I only remember bits and pieces, but suffice it to say that it was a-freaking-dorable.

And my automatic response (internally, of course)? *I wonder how Josh would have proposed to me.*

As soon as it came, I nearly collapsed with the pain of knowing his proposal will never happen. I hadn't realized until that moment that I even *wanted* to marry him.

So badly.

Because, yes … I love him.

But Evie was right. My fears about marriage and commitment are not just going to go away. I have to deal with them head-on.

And the only way to do that is walking across the room right now.

Dad shuffles his feet as he moves toward me, his shoulders hunched, cheeks sunken and unshaven. He slides into the booth across from me. I'm glad he didn't attempt a hug. That would have been awkward to say the least.

"Hi, Kayla."

"Dad." I fold my hands on the table and stare at him.

Before we can say anything more, a waitress approaches. She's a sweet young thing, probably still a teen, and she rattles off the specials—including a pumpkin milkshake—and asks if we're ready to order.

"I'll just have an iced tea, please." They don't serve alcohol here, which is good, because I'd be tempted. But I need a completely clear head to deal with the things we're going to talk about here.

"Just a water for me, thanks." Dad picks up the menu and starts scanning it as the waitress walks away. "Do you remember how you tried to order a large chocolate milkshake wherever we went when you were a kid?"

"Don't do that, Dad."

"What?" He sets down the menu and studies me.

"That thing where you try to warm me up with some story about our time together." I shake my head. "I see what you're doing and it won't work."

The waitress drops off our drinks. "Are you ready to order?"

"I'm not sure if I'm going to eat," I say. "We'll wave you down when we're ready."

Her forehead crinkles, but she nods and scurries away. Even she must sense the tension at our table.

"Kayla," my father says slowly. "I wasn't attempting to pull any tricks. Honestly."

"Fine." I wrinkle my nose, trying my best not to allow his soft tone to touch me. "I'm sure you're wondering why I asked to meet with you."

"I assumed you were just following up on my request to meet with you."

"In part, yes. I wanted to give you the floor to say what you needed to say." I pick at a spot of dried ketchup on the plastic menu in front of me. "Then it's my turn."

"That's fair."

The oldies music—something from the 1950s, maybe?—swells and dips, waiting just like I am for him to continue.

Finally, he does. "I want to apologize for leaving you, Kayla."

I stiffen at the words. Does he think that's enough? But I'm quiet. I did say I'd hear him out, after all.

He goes on. "I know my leaving hurt you. And I know you don't understand why I had to go. I tried to spare you from all of that, but maybe it's time you know the truth."

"I do know the truth. You got tired of us, tired of living in Mom's shadow, tired of her success when you couldn't get your own failing business off the ground. She was too much for you and you couldn't handle it."

His jaw goes slack. "Is that what you really think?"

I lick my lips. "It's the only thing that makes sense."

"Maybe that's your mother's 'truth,' but it isn't the whole truth—not even close. And I wasn't there to explain it to you. For that, I'm so sorry. I know it's probably something you can never forgive me for. Because despite everything, that's my biggest failure. My biggest regret." Dad starts to reach for me, then thinks better of it and drops his hand back to his menu.

"Regardless, here's my truth. Your mother was successful, that's true. As the years went on, she became more and more married to her job. I begged her to spend more time at home, but she kept saying she just needed a little more time to 'make it.'"

That does sound like her. She was always determined to succeed.

Just like you.

Dad keeps going. "She and her boss James were very close, and I always suspected … But that's neither here nor there." He waves away the accusation, but it hangs in the air all the same, soiling the image in my head, what I thought I knew. "The point is, I confronted her the night before I left. Said I'd had enough. That I was going to leave if she couldn't give our family the priority it deserved."

I remember them fighting that night. I'd been up in my room, but never heard the actual words—just their timber.

Anger. Sadness. Pain.

"So what happened?" I finally remove my straw from its paper wrapper and jam it into my tea.

"She said if I wanted to leave, I could leave. In fact, she told me if I didn't, she'd find a way to make me."

"What does that even mean?" My throat is dry, so I take a sip of tea, realizing too late that it's unsweetened.

What was that waitress thinking? I need sugar NOW.

My eyes roam the table and find a little container of sweeteners on the edge. I practically dive for a packet of sugar, rip it open, and dump it inside, dunking my straw till it's all dissolved.

My dad is watching me attack the liquid, a tinge of amusement ringing his lips.

"What?" I practically growl before taking another drink. Ahhh.

"You drank that as aggressively as Luke Skywalker drank that green milk in *The Last Jedi*." He chuckles. "Did you see that one?"

I roll my eyes. "Duh." Some part of me doesn't want him to know that I'm still a *Star Wars* fan, but I guess that ship has sailed considering he saw me at the convention dressed in full Leia garb. "Now, what do you mean, Mom said she'd find a way to make you?"

He sobers right up at the reminder of why we're really here. "I imagine she would have found a way to make me look guilty of something I didn't do. Abuse, neglect. Who knows."

"Mom may be tough, but she's not malicious."

"You don't know her like I do."

"You don't know either of us anymore," I spit out. "You forfeited that right."

He's quiet for a moment, giving me a chance to diffuse.

"Sorry. Go ahead."

He nods, sighs. "You're right. I don't know her anymore. But back then, she was bound and determined to stay in control of everything—especially you. I begged her to let me take you with me, but she said I would never get custody while she had breath in her body."

It almost sounds like Mom was abusive to him. But that's ridiculous.

Isn't it?

Also, this is the first I've heard about my dad wanting to take me with him. I tilt my head. "So why didn't you fight for me after you left?"

"I tried. But I didn't make enough to pay for a good attorney."

"Okay … so why didn't you try to see me?"

"I did, but she called the police on me a few times." He shakes his head again, pain in his eyes. "I'll give you the dates. You can check the police records."

I shiver—because I know the story he's telling me just might be true. I didn't think Mom would be that cruel, but she's always been a control freak.

And she's been controlling me this whole time.

I try one more time to indict him—to exonerate Mom. "Surely you could have fought for me if you really wanted me."

He blinks and a tear releases from his eye, trailing down his cheek. "I should have fought harder. But I didn't want to have to put you through a hearing. It would have been long, drawn out, terrible. So I waited until you turned eighteen and were on the verge of leaving home. When you could legally decide for yourself." Dad grips his water glass, his fingertips pressing into the condensation now gathering on the outside. "But by then, it was too late. She already had planted the lies in your brain, turned you into …"

"Her."

"I thought so. But …" He lifts his hand, and this

time, covers mine with it.

And, much as it is my instinct to do so, I don't move.

"I was wrong. You are much kinder, much gentler. She would never have given me a second chance, even if I wanted one. But here you are, willing to hear me out. Willing to be authentic." Dad squeezes my fist. "I know I don't deserve another chance with you, but I'm going to be bold and ask for one anyway. My life has never meant so much as when you were in it. Without you, nothing is right. Can you ever find a way to forgive me for my errors—for doing the wrong thing?"

My mouth trembles. "How do I know you won't leave me again?"

"Because I love you. And even when love has made a huge mistake, it always returns. Love keeps going, keeps trying. It never fails, not in the end." He squeezes my hand again. "I promise, baby. Nothing but death would make me leave you again."

At his words, something inside of me catches flame —not in a way that would burn down a forest, but in the way that burns gold in order to refine it.

And I find myself pulling my hand away, scooting out of the booth, and moving to his side. He wraps his arm around me and I bury my head in his chest, breathing in the long-ago scent of Old Spice. "I want to forgive you, Daddy. I'll try, okay?"

"That's all I can ask, baby. Thank you. I … I love you, sweetheart."

"I love you too."

And I do, even if I haven't quite figured out all the other emotional stuff going on inside of me. Maybe this time, though, love really will win the day.

nineteen

. . .

"EVEN WHEN LOVE *has made a huge mistake, it always returns. Love keeps going, keeps trying. It never fails, not in the end.*"

A little more than a week later, I find myself praying with everything I have that my dad's words are true.

That they can apply here, now.

My heart is threatening to run away from me as I tap a white marble countertop with swirls of gray. From the stainless steel appliances, white cabinets, and cheery yellow paint in the kitchen to the white-brick fireplace in the living room and the large windows that do indeed let in a ton of light, the house is as adorable in person as it was online.

Sure, the current owners' style is a bit too bovine in nature for my liking (they literally have cow figurines EVERYWHERE), but it doesn't take away from the craftsman's charm.

Realtor Susan Caminski circles the living room. "It

makes pretty good use of the space considering the overall square footage of the home." The woman is dressed in a long-sleeved blouse and pencil skirt, her wisps of gray hair pulled back into a bun. She shakes her head. "Didn't you say you were an attorney? Are you sure you wouldn't rather see something on the larger side?"

"Former attorney. And no, this is perfect."

Eyebrow arched, she absently touches the mantel and then brushes her thumb and forefinger together as if shaking off invisible dust. "Well, you certainly put those lawyerly skills to good use in getting the previous buyers to back out of their contract."

I grimace. That makes me sound so … underhanded. But I swear, I wasn't. I simply approached the buyers and asked if they were fully committed to the purchase or would consider looking elsewhere. They were a lovely older couple who—it turns out—believes in young love enough to gracefully bow out of the contract if another offer is made. (A home sale contingency makes this possible.)

And even though they refused to accept any gift in exchange, I fully plan to send them on an anniversary trip if this all works out. It may cost me the rest of the nest egg I built up to keep my business going, but it's worth it if Josh gets the home he wants.

If Susan's tilted head is any indication, she's awaiting some sort of reply. All I can do is shrug. "They're good people. When I explained the situation—"

"Which I still don't fully understand," Susan says.

"Why do you want this house so badly?"

Here's where I'll need Susan's full cooperation. I wasn't sure I'd get it if I told her the story over the phone. "It's not for me."

Her eyebrows raise so high they disappear underneath her bangs. "I'm listening."

"I need a huge favor from you." Then I fill her in on my plan.

By the time I'm done, she's pulling out her phone. "That's quite the story. But I'll go along—especially if you're so sure it'll net me a sale." But I can tell by her voice, she's teasing me. She'd do this even if a sale wasn't guaranteed.

Although, to be honest, I'm not so sure it is.

I have no idea how Josh will react.

Thankfully, I don't have all that long to find out. It's Tuesday, which means he's off work (I am nothing if not strategic). When Susan hangs up, she nods. "He's agreed to come over right away, though he was quite confused about why."

After I thank her for running interference, I occupy my time by walking the house, examining each and every nook and cranny to be sure—but Josh was right. This really is the perfect little house.

The perfect place to raise a family.

Aaaaaaand there go my ovaries again. But instead of a panicked tap dance, they're performing a ballet. It's smooth, bold, and confident—just like my feelings for Josh.

For the life I know I want with him.

I'm just hoping he still wants the same.

The fact we haven't spoken in exactly a month makes me doubt it. But all I can do is face my fears and move forward. To keep going, keep trying, to return even when the risk is great.

Even when rejection is highly likely.

But if I can forgive both of my parents, then anything is possible, right? (Yeah, I confronted Mom about what my dad said. She confessed that she thought she was protecting me by keeping my dad out of the picture when I was younger. It still doesn't make complete sense that she's fine with us connecting now, but I know my mother and I will never see eye to eye on everything. Still, I've chosen to forgive her because I'm sick of living in the past.)

I'm in one of the smaller bedrooms when I hear his voice. Oh man, how I've missed it. I scurry out into the living room just in time to see Susan lead Josh through the archway.

He freezes at the sight of me.

His eyes leave mine all too quickly to find Susan's. "What's going on?"

"Kayla asked me to invite you here." Susan takes a step back toward the front door. "I'm going to wait in my car. You two let me know if you need me." Then she turns on a fat one-inch heel and leaves us alone.

All too slowly—I think I age ten years—he pivots his gaze back to me. "What's going on, Kayla?"

Kayla. Not Leia.

The coolness in his tone stabs my heart like an ice pick. But I hurt him. I left. I deserve everything he has to throw at me.

Still, I will not give up without speaking my piece.

My chest aching, I blow out a breath. "Last week, I scoured the Internet for the house you showed me that night at the hotel on your phone. Found out it was already under contract—and not by you."

He crosses his arms in front of him. "I changed my mind about it."

Does that mean he's changed his mind about me too? My knees wobble and I lean against the back of the couch for support. "Well, I didn't know that. And I talked with the buyers under contract. Turns out they have a home sale contingency clause—basically, they have to sell their home before the sale of this one goes through. And if another buyer offers a better deal in the meantime, the seller can accept if the current buyers back out. Which they've agreed to do if you want to buy it."

"I'm sorry you went to all that trouble. But I don't want this place anymore."

"But … this was your dream."

He takes a step forward, then hesitates, running a hand through his hair and looking away. "Yeah. It was."

"It's not anymore?" I can't help the tremble in my voice. "I'm so sorry, Josh. Sorry that I ruined everything by leaving. I know now that I was sabotaging our relationship before it even began, because I wasn't able to handle the thought of you leaving first."

His gaze returns to me. It's still guarded, but … looser somehow.

I stand again, advancing a bit. I don't want to scare him off, but he needs to know exactly what cards I'm putting on the table. "I had it in my head that we were doomed for failure, just like my parents. That you would always see Danielle and her failures when you looked at me. That we would love each other for a little while, but not enough to stay. To fight. So I gave up early, because it was easier than giving up in five years. Or ten. Or fifteen."

Now his eyes are deep pools of sorrow, of understanding. He's hearing me, but I still don't know what he will do about it. So I keep on talking. "But Lauren and Evie showed me that we get to make our own choices. They also challenged me to deal with my past—because there was no future if I couldn't. So I did."

One more step and now he's only a foot away. "What did you do?"

"I saw my dad. We talked. And … I decided to work toward forgiving him."

"Kay, that's … amazing."

And I don't know who takes the final step—maybe we both do—but now we're standing toe to toe, my head tilted to look up into his eyes. We're physically close, but I need to say the rest to knock down the last brick in my emotional wall.

Lifting my hand to his face, I press it against his cheek. It's warm and a bit stubbly, with a few days of growth. "Josh, can you forgive me for leaving? For not realizing that I love you with every breath I have? That I want this with you? Because I do. I want the house. Marriage. Babies. All of it." And I am not one to beg, but I have to fight the instinct to get down on my knees and clasp my hands in front of me. "Please tell me it's not too late."

For a moment, he simply stares at me, lips pursed. He's thinking, processing, so I wait. Then, finally, "I know I'm not fully innocent myself in all of this. I pushed you when you weren't ready to talk about your dad, and for that I'm really sorry. I've tried to give you space the last month, like you asked, but it killed me to be apart."

So Evie and Lauren were right. "I'm glad you did. I needed it. If you'd followed me right away, I'm not sure I'd have been in a place emotionally to accept what you were saying." I allow a slow grin to cross my lips. "I'm not sure you know this about me, but I can be rather stubborn at times."

He takes hold of my hand that's on his cheek, and presses a kiss into my palm. "I do know that. And I love it about you." Then he pulls me close, wrapping his free hand around my waist—right where it belongs. "Leia, I'm pretty sure I've loved you since the first moment I met you, but that love has deepened with every moment together. Every time you've shown me another piece of your heart, every second you removed your mask enough for me to see more of you." He kisses my nose. "Every time you made a *Star Wars* reference."

We both laugh, and my heart has never felt fuller than it is now, in hearing Josh's profession.

He goes on. "I didn't even come to look at this house after our fight, because it means nothing without you. My dream isn't the house, Leia. It's you. I don't want to live inside these walls if you aren't here with me."

"Okay." I lift up on my tiptoes and brush a kiss against his mouth.

"Okay, what?" He tilts his head.

"Okay, I'll marry you."

Josh sputters out a laugh. "I don't recall asking you," he teases.

"Well, then maybe I'm asking you. Joshua Gregory, will you—"

"No."

Oh. "No?"

"You crazy woman." He shakes his head. "I mean, no, I'm not letting *you* ask *me*."

"Why not? This is the twenty-first century."

"Fine. Let's ask each other then." Then he gets down on one knee and grabs my hand.

And tears find their way to my eyes because IS THIS REALLY HAPPENING? I had no concept of this moment before now. No idea that happiness like this could ever be mine.

But now, it's all I want. Josh, and this house, and a bunch of babies to fill it. Wouldn't say no to a thriving career too, but that comes second to this. My relationships will be my priority from now on. But the beautiful thing? I know Josh will support me as I pursue my dreams.

Case in point: he's making a dream come true right now that I didn't even know I had.

"Kayla Clark—my Leia." His hand is shaking as it clasps my own. "Would you make me the happiest Jedi alive and be my princess forever?"

Oh my stars, that was the cheesiest line ever. But I am here for it.

I will always be here for it.

"You bet I will." I sink down onto my knees in front of him. "And will you marry me, Solo?"

"Yes." The word is barely out before he's tipping my chin and kissing me with the passion of a thousand suns.

And I return the heat, more than grateful for what's to come.

Before we can get too carried away—this isn't our home yet, after all—he pulls back, stands, and sweeps me up into his arms. Then he plops me down onto the couch and sits at my feet.

I giggle. "What are you doing way down there?"

He removes my sparkly wedge sandals and drops them with a thud to the floor. Then, all while watching me, he proceeds to give me the best dang foot rub of my life.

If the man hadn't just proposed to me, I'd be begging him to marry me right here and now.

But I have a lifetime of this to look forward to. Yes, there will be more fighting. There will be losses and tragedies, hardships and low points.

But there will also be *Star Wars* marathons and massages, mountains and laughter and teasing and fun.

And, if I have anything to say about it, lots and *lots* of lovemaking.

Because I love this man and he loves me—and I'm determined to choose love over fear for the rest of our lives.

epilogue

. . .

Lauren

THE HOLIDAYS AREN'T the same when you no longer spend them with family.

For me? That means they're actually fun.

No longer plastic.

They're … real.

Even if my last name is now Smith and not Everly. Even if I have to pretend that I didn't secretly check in on my baby sister via Instagram this morning—just like I do every morning. Even if I'm terrified that one of my friends will slip up someday and post a photo of me, ending my days of hiding out after social media fame and a crazy relationship stole everything from me.

But today, I'm not thinking about any of that, because it's "Friends-giving"—our pre-Thanksgiving feast that takes place the Sunday before the actual holiday.

And spending this day with my housemates isn't about making sure we have a perfect-looking table that will garner thousands of social media likes. (Which is especially ridiculous when that table has been professionally catered but we claim it's all homemade.)

It's not about smiling in front of the camera but fighting in real life.

It's also not all about dressing in the latest designer to hit the NYC boutiques and shops, so we stay at the forefront of fashion.

Which is why right now, I'm standing in our small kitchen mashing potatoes and rocking my standard yoga pants and tank top combo. I've got a nice blouse and pair of jeans laid out on my bed for the actual meal, but I probably won't take the time to wash my hair. That's why God made dry shampoo, am I right?

All around me, there's organized chaos, with Kayla and Connor vying for point person over the meal prep (Connor because he actually knows how to cook, and Kayla because she's Kayla).

Alexis is on the phone with her sister Kennedy, telling her in no uncertain terms that her taste in men is deplorable. She hangs up, disgusted, and starts pouring alcohol into the punch. Evie is standing at the kitchen island, biting her lip and doing her best to follow Connor's instructions for assembling the green bean casserole. Shelby and Eric are laughing about something in the corner while she makes her mom's cornbread dressing and he "assists" by sneaking bits of hard-boiled egg into his mouth.

Kayla's fiancé (still can't get used to saying that!) hasn't arrived yet, but he'll be here once his shift at work ends. They'll be flying out early tomorrow to spend the entire week in Oregon with his family. Since getting engaged nearly three weeks ago, the lovebirds have basically spent every spare moment together. It helps that Kayla is working at Java Awakening again (side note: Hannah apologized for her jealous behavior, and she and Kayla are working toward being friends) while slowly getting her business back on track.

Even though it's obviously not why she's marrying Josh, her engagement actually helped with her dating coach image. As annoying as it is, Instagram loves a happy couple.

See? Social media can be a good thing, when kept in context. It's all the other times, when people get obsessed with the fame, pretending to be one thing while they're actually another, not worrying how things online affect real-life … real relationships.

That's when it gets dangerous.

Not that I know anything about that. Oh wait …

Ugh, no. *Not today, past. Stay where you belong.* Because right now is about the kitchen that's crammed full with us all, with our laughter, with the heat from the stovetop, with the scent of roasted turkey and the butter I'm now whipping into the potatoes. It's about the breeze that rustles through the back screen door, refreshing and giving life to the beauty of this moment.

Yep, I'm blessed.

Even though there are times when I wish …

My eyes sting with unexpected tears. So I do the only thing I can—I reach for a distraction. Snagging my phone, I scroll to my music app and pull up 'N Sync's Christmas album.

When "Merry Christmas, Happy Holidays" comes on, all is right with my world.

Even if all of my friends are groaning.

Alexis turns from the punch and rushes me. "It's too early for Christmas music!" She's got the mixing spoon held in the air, like she's going to smack me with it.

But I dodge, too quick for her, and poke her in the sides, where I know she's ticklish. "You're such a Grinch." I giggle. "As of today, I'm declaring the Christmas music listening window officially opened."

"We agreed that wouldn't start until Thanksgiving!" Kayla singsongs from across the kitchen (which is like five feet in actuality).

"I don't know," Evie says. "It's Friends-giving. I think it should count." She does a dorky little dance move to match the music. "After all, Christmas is the best time of the year."

"I agree. Especially this year." Beside her, Connor leans down and presses a kiss against her cheek. They have a private little laugh about something.

Maybe they're thinking about their upcoming wedding. They've decided to have it just before Christmas, even if that means they have to rush to make arrangements. All of us women will be bridesmaids, and the ceremony will take place at the Japanese Friendship Garden, a place that holds significance for them both and just happened to be available.

Maybe someday, I'll have what they have, if I can ever find a man who hates the spotlight as much as I do. Until that day, I'm thankful for my people—the ones I choose.

The ones who took me in after losing everything I loved.

I clear my throat of the sudden thickness that's invading. "Thank you, Evie!" I turn up the sound on my phone and warble along with the music while my potatoes come together beautifully. My heart gets a boost when I hear my friends singing along.

"Hey, guys. Smells great in here."

I turn to find Josh stepping into the kitchen. He's smiling in that shy way of his, and he's clearly got something behind his back. When he reaches Kayla, he holds out a ring box.

She snatches it from him, opens the box, and squeals. (I still can't get over how giddy she is with him—it's weird, but also amazing.) "It wasn't supposed to be in until next week!"

All of us abandon our posts to crowd around her and see the ring they picked out a few weeks ago. Even though it's modest—Josh and Kayla are in the process of buying a house and saving for a wedding, after all—it's classy, a simple princess-cut diamond with a white gold band.

She slips it from the box onto her finger and admires it for a second, her hand outstretched while we *ooh* and *aah.* "It fits perfectly." Then she's jumping into Josh's arms and kissing him senseless.

Eric and Connor clear their throats and turn away, grinning, while the rest of us giggle and elbow one another.

This right here—the light, the happiness, the camaraderie—is perfect.

My *life* is perfect.
Even if it is a lie.

WANT to learn more about Lauren's past—and what's in store for her future? Check out her story in *Saving the Secret Prince*.

Thanks for reading Josh and Kayla's story. If you enjoyed it, would you consider leaving a review?

Also, if you'd like to join my newsletter for updates on my other books, book recommendations, deals, giveaways, and more, sign up at www.KristinCanary.com/subscribe.

sneak peek

Saving the Secret Prince

There's one thing you need to know about me—one very important detail that is much more important than who my mother is or what I do for a living or my last name.

Ready for it?

Here we go—

Oops. Got distracted there for a minute by the lyrics in my head. This happens more than you might think. Ahem.

Where was I? Right.

The thing you need to know about me is that I just might be the biggest lover of the '90s boy band 'N Sync who has ever existed.

That's right, I said it. Ever.

My eternal love of the Fab Five is how I find myself at the San Diego arena on a Friday night, cheeks wet and heart full. Despite being surrounded for the last three hours by thousands of screaming thirty-something women pretending like their hormones haven't yet regulated, I'm still sighing in sweet, sweet contentment. For one night and one night only, we have all been released from the bonds of the mid-life doldrums and allowed to act like total preteens drooling over the latest issue of *Teen Bop* magazine.

Because that's what happens when 'N Sync finally does the reunion concert you've been waiting for all your life.

After swiping away the tears of joy that rolled down my face during the closing number, I sling my arm around my housemate, Shelby Phillips. "That was the best thing ever. Forget marriage and babies—I think I can really and truly die happy now."

Her short blonde hair bobs as she shakes her head at me and smiles. "It was good, Lauren."

The noise level around us starts to die off as the audience continues its exit from the concert venue.

"Shelbs, that was not just good. That"—I gesture toward the now-deserted stage, where five of the best vocal talents in history just sang, danced, and made love to the crowd together—"was pure genius. Did you see when Justin flew in from above?

"You mean JT?"

"He will always and forever be only Justin to me." I place a hand over my heart dramatically. "They pretended like he couldn't make it and then BAM—there he was. It was magic."

Shelby grabs my hand and squeezes it. "It was fun seeing you so excited."

Once again, my twenty-five-year-old housemate has proven her sweet nature by letting me drag her to a concert she cares nothing about. Give her a good old-fashioned musical and she'd have the same giddy look I'm sure I'm wearing, but I guess pop music doesn't do it for her. "You're just too young to fully appreciate the glory that was Justin's bleached curly-sue locks or the thrill of learning the choreography to *Bye Bye Bye* behind the bleachers after school."

By this time, most of our row has cleared out. Next to me, the large dude with the surprisingly high-pitched falsetto who knew every single word of every single song (props to him, man) turns and shuffles out behind a green-haired female with a T-shirt featuring Joey Fatone's face. Her style hardly matches my own boring brown locks, skinny jeans, and green long-sleeved blouse, but that just proves how 'N Sync brings people together.

Le sigh. They really are the best.

We follow the lingering crowd off the main arena floor and into the hallway. "I need to stop at the restroom really quick if that's okay," Shelby says.

"Yeah, of course." The large windows of the arena show a gorgeous moon and twinkling stars outside. While Shelby slips into the restroom line, I pull my phone from my purse. Absently, I check my email. There's nothing much new, just a company-wide message from my boss, Jen, at New Heights Gym about holiday promotions we've got going on. Not surprising with Christmas only three weeks and one day away.

I get that familiar pinch in my chest, the one that

always comes when I think about the holidays and how far away my family is. About how that's my own choice, made out of necessity, survival.

In order to preserve who I am—who I want to be—I had to escape.

But that doesn't mean I don't think about my mom and sister, Samantha. That never stops. It's why I regularly stalk their social media pages.

Before I can stop myself, I navigate to the one social media site I'm a member of. The first thing I see is my own profile and a cascade of photos I've taken. Some women keep written diaries, but my journal is this digital photo album that no one else sees—because I don't allow any followers.

Flipping to Sam's page, I smile when I see a selfie of her cheek to cheek with her best friends at some sort of nightclub. She's cut her brown hair chin length and her eyes are done all smoky-like. In her mid-twenties, she's so beautiful, so full of life. Or that's how it appears in the photos, anyway.

I wish I knew for sure.

But after leaving the way I did, I don't have a right to ask for details about her life. We keep our relationship to occasional texting. That was my choice five years ago—and I don't know how to change it now. All I can do is pray that our mother hasn't dug her claws into Sam, that the independent streak I've always admired in my sister has held strong. That she hasn't let Mom's fame change her.

"Ready to go?"

I startle and nearly drop my phone at Shelby's

sudden appearance by my side. Clearing my throat, I shove my phone back into my purse. "Yep." Then I take off at a quick clip, as if I can escape the demons of my past.

"Whoa, you okay?" Shelby hurries to keep up as we dodge people—people everywhere.

"Of course." And why shouldn't I be? "We just experienced a once-in-a-lifetime event. I'm going to tell my kids about that concert." If I can ever meet a decent guy, that is. Not that I've really tried. Oh sure, I go on dates now and again, but nothing ever sticks.

After the fiasco with Danny, I'm not too eager to try again with someone new. Of course, next time I'll make sure I don't fall for some hotshot who's in the public eye.

We finally make our way past the long line of concertgoers waiting to buy merch and emerge into the crisp night air.

"Brr." Shelby tugs on her adorable pink trench coat and burrows down. "I know this is probably nothing compared with the East Coast, but this California girl is cold."

It used to be funny to me, how people here bust out the scarves and coats when it turns sixty-five out. Of course, San Diego is this strange SoCal pocket where things can get chillier than you might expect. But it's almost always *at least* fifty degrees around the holidays.

And while I do miss snow at Christmas, there's something about the sparkling sand of the beaches in winter that makes this feel more like home—more inviting—than New York ever did.

Now, the cold December air feels amazing on my skin after the proximity to so many bodies in the arena. Or maybe I'm still just heated from all my internal friction after seeing my sister's photo. Either way, I crave the open air and can't imagine climbing back into a vehicle right now. "How do you feel about a walk?"

Shelby's nose scrunches. "Like, right now?" She blows into her hands.

I link my arm with hers. "It's the weekend and the night is young. Come on. I'll keep you warm." Some might call me impulsive, but I like to think of it as seizing the day. "If I remember right, there's a cute coffee shop not that far from here. I'll buy you one of those fancy drinks you like." And get myself a hot chocolate.

"All right." The light from the many streetlamps illuminating the concrete and asphalt obscures the pretty sky. "But won't Josh and Kayla feel like you're cheating on Java Awakening?" she teases.

I laugh as we walk toward the sidewalk on the far end of the parking lot. "I think they'll understand. I've only been working there a week, after all."

"I don't know how you fit it all in. Gym instructor, teacher's aide, barista. You're like Superwoman."

Shrugging, I toss my hair over my shoulder. "The jobs pay the bills, and I like the variety."

Reaching the sidewalk, we turn north, away from the lengthy line of cars waiting to get on the main road that will take them to the freeway. Instead, we take the long way. It's not as populated with a bit less light, but we're together, so I'm not too worried about weirdos approaching us.

"So, how is it working with the newlyweds?" Shelby's teeth chatter slightly. "I am so happy for Kayla, but I wish we could have been at their wedding."

Kayla, one of our former housemates, showed up married last weekend after a Thanksgiving trip to visit her fiancé Josh's family in Oregon. Apparently they made a pit stop in Vegas after Josh's mom peppered her with questions about the wedding. That, plus the fact that a wedding is expensive—they just bought a house and Kayla is running a fledgling dating coach business—led to their decision to marry quickly.

I inhale, the scent of the ocean not far away. There are so many things I love about living here—the food, my friends, not to mention the freedom to be who I want to be without fear that it'll be documented and twisted—and the beach ranks high on the list. "I know, Shelbs. But Kayla and Josh are happy and that's all that matters, right?"

"Of course." A pause. "I hope someday to be as happy as them. And Evie and Connor, too."

Our other former housemate, Evie, is marrying her fiancé in two and a half weeks, just days before Christmas. We're all bridesmaids, and it's going to be beautiful. I can't wait to bust out my phone and take photos when no one is watching.

"You will. Keep the faith." Up ahead, I spot a lone man striding down the sidewalk toward us and talking on his phone—loudly—but he's too far away for me to hear what he's saying. A black hoodie is pulled over his head, obscuring his face in the dim light.

I return my attention to Shelby and try to effect a casual tone. "Who knows. Maybe we've already met the men we're going to marry and just don't know it yet."

All of us think Shelby and her best friend, Eric, would be perfect together. The only ones who don't seem to see it are Shelby and Eric themselves. But it always makes Shelby blush when we tease her about it, so I think there's more to the story.

"I—"

Shelby's comment is interrupted by the shouts of the man on the phone. Now he's stopped at a crosswalk and gesticulating wildly. A single car passes down the street, a reminder that this area is rather deserted. No one would hear us scream if the guy decided to turn and attack.

I halt, tugging on Shelby's arm. "Maybe we should go a different way."

"I'm sorry for leaving like that, all right?" The man— who is speaking in a delectable British-like accent—rubs his forehead and the hood of his sweatshirt falls away.

And darn it all if I don't lose feeling in my toes. Everything goes tingly and I feel like God must have spent a little more time on him, if you know what I'm saying. The harmony plays in my mind and I nearly break out into a song. Seriously.

Maybe it's the lamplight shining down on him, but he resembles some sort of sleek demigod—a savory Superman-slash-Thor sandwich.

I mean, sure, I can't see the exact details of his face,

except for a dark beard covering his square jaw and chiseled cheekbones, but there's something almost elegant about his posture. He commands attention and I wonder what other superpowers he might possess in addition to extreme hotness.

Thankfully, he doesn't notice my gawking. Doesn't notice Shelby or me at all, it seems.

Blowing out a breath, SuperThor rubs a hand along the back of his neck and stares at the street. "I just needed to get away for a bit."

Who is he talking to? A boss? A friend? Oh no. A girlfriend. Is it a girlfriend?

Of course it's a girlfriend. A man like THAT definitely has a girlfriend. Or wait, a wife. Is he wearing a ring? I look for a flash of gold or silver on his finger, but it's too dark.

Girl, you've officially lost it.

"Lauren," Shelby whispers. "Should we go?"

"Um—" Yes. Probably.

But before I can make a decision one way or another, it's made for me. SuperThor begins to cross the street.

Bye bye bye. I'll always remember you, SuperThor.

Shelby and I start walking again, but suddenly the road fills with headlights as a car careens around the corner.

And SuperThor just keeps chattering and yelling into his phone, apparently unaware that his life should be flashing before his probably-delicious eyes right about now.

I gasp, drop Shelby's arm, and sprint toward him like it's *my* life that depends on it. "Look out!"

At my shout, he turns to me. "What?" Then he sees the car and his eyes widen.

Just before the car connects with him—or me—I fling my body at him. We both fly toward the opposite sidewalk and land with an *oomph* as our heads knock together.

Tires squeal, and I should be concerned, but most of my attention is stuck on his eyes, the color of which I can't quite seem to grasp in the darkness. But they're piercing, I'll give him that.

"Are you all right, love?"

Love. He called me love. I laugh and inhale sharply. Wait, why am I giggling like a schoolgirl? But oh my gosh, he definitely came from heaven because the dude smells divine—like jasmine and cedar and bergamot and sandalwood, all wrapped up in one lovely package.

Merry Almost Christmas to me.

That's when I realize—why does my brain feel so stupidly slow?—that I'm lying on top of him on the asphalt.

"Sorry," I say, but I don't move. I'm not sure I can. My head is about to split into two.

"No worries." He shifts me gently so I'm level with him on the ground. One of his arms is still beneath my body and his eyes continue to study me. "Are you okay?"

Ambulance sirens whine in the background, getting louder and louder by the second. Why is there an ambulance? We're all fine here.

"Yep. Just fine. Fine, fine, fine." I lay my head down

against his Thor-like chest and snuggle into the crook of his arm. "I take back what I said. *Now* I can die happy."

I giggle again, but the laughter sends a sharp pain through my skull. "Ow." Then, I close my eyes.

The last thing I hear before everything goes black is the whisper of a promise—"No one's dying tonight, love."

books by kristin canary

California Dreamin' Series

Enamoring Her Amnesic Ex (prequel)

Loving the Ladies' Man

Desiring His Dating Coach

Saving the Secret Prince

Belonging With Her Best Friend

Engaging the Office Enemy

Needing the Next-Door Neighbor

Hallmark Beach Series

Beachside Kisses With My Bodyguard

about the author

Kristin is a wife and boy mom who functions best on peach tea and cookie dough ice cream. A desert dweller, she always has her eye on the next trip to a beach somewhere—and if she can't travel there in person, then you'd better believe she's going to write about it. Kristin is never fully satisfied with a movie, TV show, or book without a hefty dose of romance in it, and she's grateful to be living a true-life love story with her own crazy little family. Connect with her at KristinCanary.com.

facebook.com/kristincanary
instagram.com/kristincanaryauthor

www.ingramcontent.com/pod-product-compliance
Lightning Source LLC
Chambersburg PA
CBHW021127190726
48288CB00008B/2529